MASSACRE CANYON

MASSACRE CANYON

Jackson Cole

GUNSMOKE

First published in the US by Pyramid Books

This hardback edition 2012
by AudioGO Ltd
by arrangement with
Golden West Literary Agency

ISBN 978 1 445 88688 6

British Library Cataloguing in Publication Data available.

Printed and bound in Great Britain by
MPG Books Group Limited

Chapter I

"CAPITAN, death sits upon those hills. Death, and terror."

"What do you mean, Manuel?"

The old Mexican glanced nervously about, lowered his voice.

"It is as I say, Capitan, death is there—death comes from there."

Ranger Jim Hatfield glanced from old Manuel's leathery countenance to where, far to the northwest, the Tinaja Hills were a dark wall against the skyline, a ragged, spired, and fanged wall of hard blues and purples with here and there the raw, red gash of a dry wash or the black blotch of a canyon mouth.

Between the hills and the river town at the edge of which Hatfield sat his magnificent golden sorrel horse, were mile upon mile of emerald billows that were luxurious rangeland. Here and there were those strange, arid patches of desert encountered in Southwest Texas, upon which gnarled greasewood and grotesque cactus forms struggled for existence. In the main, however, the smiling earth was clothed in a garment of richest green, which the little streams edged with silver.

Hatfield turned back to the peon, who was regarding him with a curious mixture of doglike adoration and awe.

"Just what do you mean, amigo?" he repeated.

Again old Manuel glanced nervously about. There was no one within hearing, but his voice sank almost to a whisper.

"Formerly, Capitan, our young men went there," he said, "went there to hunt of the game and to dig the

5

herbs found only in the hills. For many years this was done. The young men journeyed to the hills, and returned with full bags or loaded burros. Then suddenly there was a change. The young men who went into the hills did not return. Others went seeking them, and did not return. Others, armed and vigilant, rode into the hills and found—nothing. So our people went no more to the hills. And then, and then, Capitan, came the riders of the night, and he!"

"He?"

"Si, Capitan. He came, and the riders who forced men of the river towns to go with them. Work they were promised, and wages, but the wages were death!"

Hatfield's gray eyes narrowed. He knew something of the artifices of Mexican mine and ranch owners when they found themselves in need of labor. They raided little settlements where the peons lived and took away the simple laborers whether they desired to go or not. Well, that might be the custom below the Line, but on the north bank of the Rio Grande it was something else again. These people, Mexican by blood though they might be, were citizens of Texas, and as such entitled to all the protection a great state could give. Patiently he set out to get to the bottom of the matter.

"Just who is the fellow you called 'he,' Manuel? Is he a big ranch owner, a haciendado?"

The old Mexican hesitated, sweat beading his swart cheeks. His whisper held a hissing note when he spoke—

"He, Capitan, is El Hombre sin cara!"

"'The man without a face,'" Hatfield translated, wondering just what was actually meant by what appeared to be a Spanish figure of speech. He knew too much of the flowery land of mañana and its people to place a literal meaning upon such expressions.

"You mean you don't see his face, or that he has scars on it?" he asked.

Manuel nodded vaguely.

"Si," he said, "el cicatriz, the scar—si, he is without face."

Hatfield let it go at that.

"And the men who ride with him?" he asked. Manuel hissed venomously.

"*Capitan*, they are devils!"

"Well, I suppose you feel that way about it anyhow," he admitted. "You say none of these men ever come back?"

Manuel's eyes shifted nervously. He wet his shrunken lips. He hesitated, his wrinkled face working with the mental effort of reaching some momentous decision. Finally he burst into vigorous speech.

"*Si, Capitan, si!* Some have come back—to die! Wait, *Capitan*," as Hatfield was about to interrupt. "Wait, there is even now one here who came back. You would see that one, *Capitan?*"

"Sure! I'd like to hear what he has to say about it."

"You will not hear, *Capitan*," Manuel replied cryptically, "but you shall see. Come!"

With the golden horse pacing slowly behind him, he led the way to a tiny adobe a few hundred yards distant. He knocked on the door, mumbled something in Spanish and motioned for the Ranger to dismount.

Leaving the golden horse tied to the evening breeze, Hatfield followed the Mexican through the door, which had swung open to reveal a shadowy interior. He had to bend his head slightly to avoid striking the crown of his broad-brimmed hat against the low arch.

For a moment Hatfield paused to accustom his eyes to the change of light; at first he could make out nothing other than shadows. Then one of the shadows resolved into an ancient crone who looked more Indian than Mexican. On the far side of the room was a bed, and on the bed lay something that writhed feebly and gave forth a gabbling sound. Hatfield approached the bed.

"Here," said Manuel, "is one of those who came back."

Jim Hatfield bent over the bed and stared at what lay there. Once it had been a man. Now it was a *thing!* A *thing* that writhed slowly and steadily with the movement of a torpid snake. More than anything else Hatfield could call to mind, that awful, timeless motion suggested the slithery convolutions of a reptile. It seemed a movement of flabby flesh alone; as if there was no bony structure to support the shrunken muscles. Hollow eye sockets stared up unseeingly. From the festering, toothless opening that had been a mouth drooled the raucous gabbling.

Feeling suddenly sick, Hatfield straightened up and took an involuntary step back from the shuddery horror. His feeling of loathing was submerged in a wave of pity that was instantly followed by a gust of red rage.

"What did they do to him?" he demanded.

Old Manuel shrugged his shoulders with Latin expressiveness, and resorted to that universal Mexican phrase that dismisses the inexplicable.

"Quien sabe! Who knows!"

Hatfield studied the figure on the bed. In the course of his years of Ranger service, he had encountered more than one of the ingenious tortures that were the product of Spanish and Indian imagination, but this was something new.

Poison of some kind, he hazarded. Again overwhelming rage surged through his being. Rage directed toward the perpetrators of this hideous cruelty.

Why had they returned the pitiful remnant to its native village? To Hatfield, familiar with and understanding the devious workings of the furtive Indo-Latin mind, the reason was clear. Here was a subtle warning from the patron, an example of the fate that would overtake others who resisted his will or had the temerity to object to labor not of their own choice. Hatfield grimly resolved upon an interview with the patron in question, once he had established his identity, that would not be comfortable for said patron.

Establishing his identity, the Ranger felt, should not be difficult. From what old Manuel said, it appeared that the recruited labor was used somewhere in the Tinaja Hills or adjacent thereto. It would be largely a matter of elimination. There were several Mexican-owned cattle outfits in this section of Texas. Also, somewhat farther west, a number of mines operated by Mexicans or Texans of Mexican descent.

"Somebody's raisin' hell in the river towns," Captain Bill McDowell had told his ace Ranger when he handed him his latest assignment. "Complaints has been driftin' in—the kind we always get from the towns. You can't make head or tail of 'em, except that there's trouble. Revolution, perhaps, down below the Line, with some two-peso bandit callin' himself a general and whooping 'liberty!' Meaning liberty for him to do some choice robbing and murdering, with a lot of poor misguided devils to pull the chestnuts out of the fire for him, and get their fingers almighty burned in the pulling. That kind always stirs up a ruckus in the villages on the north bank of the river, if they can. That's liable to be the trouble. Amble over that way, Jim, and have a look-see. You can cool things down before they get well under way. We haven't a troop to spare to bust up a Border war in this section right now, or anyways soon, by the looks of things over east and up in the Panhandle. I'm expecting orders to take the boys up there most any day."

Riding through the little river towns, picking up what crumbs of information he might, Hatfield had run across old Manuel Cardenas, whom he had contacted before in the course of his Ranger activities. Manuel, albeit somewhat reluctantly, and evidently much afraid, had given the Ranger his first real clue as to what was disturbing the villages.

"You say this isn't the first man who has come back from the hills?" Hatfield asked suddenly.

"Two others have come back," Manuel replied.

Hatfield shot a shrewd question at the old Mexican.

"And each time, right after they have come back, there was a raid by the night riding jiggers you spoke of, si?"

"Sangre de Cristo! how does el Capitan know that?" Manuel exclaimed in startled surprise.

Hatfield countered with another question.

"And each time, they took men away with them, is it not so, *amigo?*"

"Si, Capitan, but—"

"And that means they'll be coming back again soon, now, eh?"

Old Manuel wet his lips nervously. "*Capitan*," he began desperately.

"Don't let it worry you, old timer," Hatfield interrupted gently. "I have a notion this is the last time they will ride this way."

Glancing into the Ranger's eyes, now cold as brittle winter sunlight, old Manuel thought so too.

"*El Lobo Solitario!* The Lone Wolf!" he murmured under his breath.

Chapter II

Manuel Cardenas lived with his lithe, flashing-eyed daughter in a comfortable· little cabin near the outskirts of the town. Rosa, the daughter, kept house for her father who was an expert powder man and earned a good living in one of the American owned mines just south of the river. She heartily seconded Manuel's suggestion that Hatfield make their home his headquarters.

That night, sitting on his bunk in the little room under the eaves, enjoying a quiet smoke, Hatfield's mind turned to the dying man in the adobe hut. The Lone Wolf had interviewed the local doctor. The medical man had admitted his inability to catalogue the mysterious ailment.

"Never before, señor, have I encountered such symptoms," he answered Hatfield's questions with Latin courtesy. "Poison? Perhaps, but if so, a drug unknown to me. Some astoundingly violent irritant. How applied, I cannot say. If it is disease, it is one unknown to this land of ours."

Jim Hatfield, who had had a couple of years in college before the death of his father, subsequent to the loss of the elder Hatfield's ranch and other business reverses, had traveled extensively and had, during a summer vacation, made a trip to the Orient. His memory stirred with some things he had seen in that breeding place of plagues.

"How about something of the leprosy sort, or bubonic, doctor?" he asked.

The old doctor shrugged. "It is possible," he admitted. "In the far eastern countries are sicknesses of which we of the western world know little. This is not leprosy, of a certainty, but it might well be some kindred ailment. I thought of that, and searched my books for possible information, and found nothing I would be willing to apply conclusively. Still, I admit the possibility, although I lean to some virulent poison. This man? He will die before another night has passed."

Hatfield nodded. In his mind a plan was taking shape which he did not mention to the doctor. He had, in fact, resolved, if it were possible to do so, to send the ravished corpse to a medical college for dissection and study. Well, that could wait until the poor devil actually cashed in his chips.

It was a night of white moonlight that paled the stars to needlepoints of silver in the blue-black velvet tapestry of the sky. There was no wind that could be heard, but a tiny whispering among the grasses told of the silvery passing of unseen feet—the kiss of the dew, the caress of the cooling air.

Sounds travel far on such a night and Hatfield heard the click of fast hoofs while they were still a very long way off.

Others heard the sound, also. When the Lone Wolf stepped from the cabin and approached the little plaza about which the village centered, he saw huddled, furtive figures that had crept from the shelter of hut and adobe and were gazing fearfully into the dark mystery of the north. The north, where those ominous black hills fanged against the moon drenched sky.

Hatfield heard mutterings from the tense groups. Over and over sounded a phrase—"*Los caballeros! Los cabelleros de la noche!*"

"The riders!" he repeated in English. "The riders of the night! Yes, it's they all right. Well, I reckon this is the showdown!"

Guns loose in their holsters, he waited, his tall figure looming gigantic in the shadow. His gray eyes glinting in the shadow of his wide hat.

Louder and louder grew the pulsing hoofbeats. They drummed the tense air until it quivered with the castaneting vibration. Individual beats merged to a steady roll that crashed to abrupt silence as a tight group swung into the plaza and cruel Mexican bits jerked the sweating horses to a halt.

For a long moment the silence endured, a silence unbroken save for the small jingle of bridle metal and the breathing of the blown horses. Utterly motionless, the grim riders sat their saddles, *sombreros* drawn low, *serapes* muffled high about their chins.

From the huddle of *peons* arose a tremulous sigh, as if, at a concerted signal, each individual had exhaled a trembling breath. Followed a nervous shifting of feet.

Still the mounted group maintained a stony silence. To Hatfield the studied intent was plain: the eerie moonlight, the furtive, questing shadows, the sinister, motionless group—all could be counted upon to strike terror into and numb the minds of the *peons*, who, despite the infusion of Spanish blood, were at heart still *Indios*, with all the Indian's superstitions and unreasoning fear of the unknown. The dark faced men and women of the river villages had no lack of physical courage. They could face death with stoical indifference, endure the most terrific pain in uncomplaining silence. But here was something they did not understand, therefore terrible. Their spirit was sapped, their resistance weakened.

A voice rang out, harsh, peremptory, speaking the Spanish the villagers understood.

"The *alcalde*," commanded the voice. "Let the *alcalde* stand forth!"

The trembling mayor of the village shuffled forward with furtive glances toward the speaker. Hatfield's glance was also upon the man, who sat his horse a little in front of his followers. And as he gazed, the Lone Wolf's eyes dilated and muscles rippled along the line of his lean jaw. Unbelievingly he peered through the moon drenched shadows. The man apparently *had no face!*

No face in the real sense of the word. What could be seen between low drawn hat brim and high muffling *serape* appeared a scarred shapelessness, a mere blurring of features without any definite lines other than the blaze of deepset eyes. Hatfield would have given much for clear sunlight at the moment.

The faceless man spoke again, in clear, ringing accents.

"Ten men are wanted," he said, "ten men to work at a good wage. The *patron* commands."

The old mayor bowed his white head, then raised it valiantly.

"Señor," he protested, "it is ill for our young men to ride north. Those who came back do not come back as —men."

The leader of the mounted group said nothing. His hand moved and the lash of a long quirt snapped across the mayor's face. Blood spurted. The old *alcalde* reeled back.

Jim Hatfield took a long stride forward. He shouldered the dazed mayor aside and faced the group from which a mutter went up. His voice rang out, edged with steel—

"Get off those horses and line up, all of you. You're under arrest! In the name of the State of Texas!"

The mounted men could see little of his face, save the glint of his eyes. But on his breast gleamed the silver-circled star of the Rangers and his voice was laden with authority. There was a crawling moment of silence. And then the Lone Wolf's hands moved with the speed of light. He had caught the flicker of shifting steel.

He shot the gun drawer before the latter could pull trigger, sending him crashing from the saddle.

Instantly there was a concerted roar of gunfire. Flame streamed from the muzzles of Hatfield's long Colts. Answering flame flickered from the dark group, like lightning along the edges of a storm cloud.

The *peons* fled in wailing terror. Old Manuel Cardenas alone hauled an ancient horse pistol from beneath his serape and banged away until the hammer clicked on an exploded cap. Reeling backward from a terrific blow on the chest, Hatfield steadied himself and took deliberate aim.

In the space of three long breaths, the fight was over. The raiders, quirting their maddened horses, fled from the death blast of those unerring guns. Six of their number lay silent in the dust of the plaza. A seventh reeled in his saddle as the Lone Wolf sent his last bullet screeching after them.

Graying face set like stone, blood gushing from his mouth and pulsing from the small blue hole in his left breast, Jim Hatfield walked stiffly forward. Beside a motionless figure whose glazing eyes glared unseeingly into the moon drenched sky, he paused, peering down into the distorted face. Something about those dead eyes, something that the pain-twisted glance of a man of less keen perception would have missed, caused his own eyes to narrow. For an instant he stared unbelievingly, slowly holstering his empty guns. Then his tall form swayed and crumpled, to lie silently beside the dead man in the dust.

Old Manuel stopped trying to reload his clumsy weapon and stumbled forward. His daughter Rosa came running on swift feet. Others gathered around. Manuel made a hurried examination. The old doctor arrived a moment later. He and Manuel exchanged glances over the bared chest; Manuel shook his head sadly.

"He will die!"

The old doctor nodded with reluctant agreement. Rosa's shapely lips set tight, her dark eyes blazed with resentment.

"He will not die!" she declared. "Help me with him, indolent ones. Men have lived before now that you said would die!"

They got him into the cabin and laid him on a couch. With skillful bandages and an infusion of herbs known only to the women of the *Indios*, the Mexican girl stopped the terrible bleeding. With the gray light of dawn, the Ranger lay white and motionless, but still breathing, although so lightly that the rise and fall of his broad chest could scarce be noted. Rosa and her father looked questioningly into each other's faces. Finally the girl spoke.

"There is but one chance, *padre*," she said. Old Manuel nodded his understanding.

"*Si*, the Señor Page," he said.

Rosa's eyes, dark-circled from strain and lack of sleep, were worried.

"Do you think he will lend his help?" she asked. "This man is not of our blood."

"I can but try—no man can do more," replied Manuel. "Prepare food while I saddle my *caballo*. I ride at once."

North by east, old Manuel rode, toward the big Cross P ranch, the owner of which was a man from the east, Nelson Page, who had purchased the spread and come to live there less than two years before.

Nelson Page was a recluse who seldom left his house. He was well thought of, although he held scant converse with his neighbors and but little was known concerning him. A former westerner who had lived many years in the east, he had decided, so rumor said, to spend his declining years in the borderland country.

His passion appeared to be Indians and Mexicans; he had befriended many, and turned none from his door who came seeking help. Likewise, it was said, he had little love for men of his own race. The story was that he had had much trouble in the more civilized east, had been defrauded by trusted business associates and had suffered severely from wounds inflicted by white criminals.

A Chinese doctor had saved him from death and earned his gratitude.

Old Manuel reached the Cross P ranchhouse before midday and was admitted at once. Nelson Page received him in the lofty, curtained room which was his library and study. The master of the Cross P was seated behind a huge dark desk, a somber hued blanket draped across his legs. The big shadowy room was hung with black velvet. A student's lamp cast its restful brilliance upon the gleaming top of the book-covered desk.

Page, leaning comfortably back in the shadow, his white, perfectly formed features devoid of expression, gazed at the old Mexican with inscrutable dark eyes. Beside him stood a gigantic Chinese—Tsiang, the physician, his constant companion. Page listened to Manuel's plea. He glanced at the Chinese doctor, who nodded his magnificently shaped head.

"I will go, and do what I may," said the Chinese, speaking in precise unaccented English. "It sounds hopeless, but I will go."

"It is well," said Page in his sonorous, vibrant voice. "Come to me always when you need help," he told Manuel.

"Gracias, señor, gracias!" exclaimed the peon. "Ai! a man, that!" he added as Tsiang led him from the room. Page stared after him, his face still expressionless.

Tsiang was far from expressionless as, the flame of the sunset streaming across the cabin floor, he gazed into the still face of Jim Hatfield.

"This man is of white blood," he said accusingly to Manuel. "You know the feeling of the master. You led him to believe the man to be of your own kin."

"I said he was as my own son," defended the peon. "And, señor, he is. Life itself I owe to this man."

The Chinese brooded over the white face of the Ranger. Old Manuel, his own face drawn with anxiety, watched him. Rosa's lips moved as in prayer. Tsiang seemed to weigh values and consequences in the balance of his inscrutable mind. Finally, decision showed on his gaunt countenance.

"Light," he said, "much light—all that can be procured—and hot water." He snapped open his black leather case, displaying an array of gleaming instruments. With swift, sure hands he laid bare the Lone Wolf's broad breast. His obsidian eyes mirrored fleeting approval of the skillful bandages, the aromatic poultice. He turned to the lithe Mexican girl.

"Your work?" he asked. Rosa bowed her dark head.

Tsiang spoke, precisely, unemotionally, as was his wont—

"If the man lives, and I believe now that he will, it is to this woman he owes his life."

Rosa's shapely head remained bowed, but her great liquid eyes glowed like exultant stars.

Chapter III

Night brooded over the great Regal ranch like a nesting bird. Under the dark mantle, banded with shadows and sewn with stars, the vast reaches of rolling rangeland were a blue-purple mystery a-whisper with the music of the wind. Hill and crag and beetling cliff loomed gigantic and unreal, their gaunt outlines beveled and softened. Canyons were ebon slashes with slightly grayed edges—edges furred, as it were, with the seepings of light that filtered down through the timeless immensities of the inverted sky bowl. Patches of desert were like to chalky scrapings from bleached bones and appeared faintly phosphorescent with stored-up star shimmer or turgid dregs of long dead sunshine.

From the stately Rio Grande to the sinister battlements of the Tinaja Hills, and on into their wild fastnesses, stretched the great ranch, as large, almost, as a small eastern state. Its vast herds roamed through brake and canyon and spired hills. Wild of eye and long of horn were those ganado. Sleek and fat, too, for the curly mesquite, the succulent buffalo grass, and the equally nutritious and even hardier bunch grass were rich with the juices of the hot Texas sunlight and the sweet rains of the desert country.

Sentinels guarded the borders of the ranch, sturdy sentinels of burr oak or other hardy woods. Line on line they marched over hill and swale and swelling slope, embedded deep in the soil, rising to the height of a tall man. And from post to post stretched taut strands of barbed wire. For the Regal was a fenced ranch, despite its vast extent. A fenced ranch in the very heart of the open range!

Don Sebastian Gomez owned the Regal. "El Rey" he had named it, when first he came north from old Mexico and bought the lordly acres. Common local usage had changed "The King" to Regal, and Don Sebastian, a courtly gentleman, had bowed to the preference of his neighbors, and he himself always referred to his property as the Regal. His brand was the Lazy R.

That was before his feud with the McCoys. Old Anse McCoy, head of the clan, hated everything Mexican. A veteran of the Mexican War and nearing ninety, that hate dated from a bullet that had left him a limping cripple. He resented the coming of the *hidalgo* into Texas, although the war in question was by that time remembered only by a handful of white-bearded veterans. Venomous as a broken-backed rattler, the old hellion managed to kick up a vicious row over little or nothing. Furthermore, he embroiled certain of his friends and acquaintances.

The upshot of the matter was that Don Sebastian, burning with a sense of injustice, fenced his range and withdrew from all intercourse with his American-born neighbors. Old Anse learned that Spanish hate could be as barbed and deadly as anything that ever came out of the Kentucky mountains. Don Sebastian's *vaqueros*, lithe, dark-faced young men, differing very little from the lean cowboys of Texas, rode his broad acres with instructions to eject summarily all trespassers. In a country where men still carried the "law" largely on their hips, this edict did not make for sweetness and peace.

Old Anse McCoy feared nothing he had ever seen or heard tell of, and Don Sebastian, a better educated man, knew even more things not to be afraid of.

At first, sentiment had been pretty well divided, but when Don Sebastian fenced his range, feeling turned more and more against him. The cattlemen of Western Texas resented barbed wire and had little use for anybody who employed it.

So the proud Spaniard withdrew to his vast estate and became very much a recluse. But still things were not peaceful and unrest continued in the district.

The Regal ranch, among other things, boasted the best hunting in the district. Game abounded in the Tinaja Hills and that portion encircled by the strands of rusty wire had become in the nature of a sanctuary for the wild life. Venturesome young ranchers slipped over the fence and came back, sometimes with fat bags. At other times they came back in very much of a hurry, bullets whistling over their heads and the yells of Don Sebastian's vaqueros ringing in their ears. More than one had know the sting of quirt or expertly wielded lariat. Once a soundly quirted cowboy cut loose with his shotgun and peppered his tormentors with bird-shot, and received a severe drubbing in return. Such happenings added fuel to the fires of resentment burning on both sides of the barbed wire.

"There'll a killin' come outa it yet, mark my word for it," old timers took to saying. Others glowered blackly toward the great spread. "That damn greaser ain't got no bus'ness comin' up here fencin' land," was a frequently heard remark.

"Yuh can't be 'zactly right and call Don Sebastian a greaser," fair-minded individuals would point out.

"Anythin' what comes from t'other side the River is a greaser," was the obstinate reply. "If this keeps on, somethin's gonna happen over there what'll set this hull deestrict to blazin', yuh see if it don't!"

Walt Hardy and his brother Tom knew just what the situation was, that night of whistling wind under a moon-drenched sky, when they slipped through the fence up near the first ragged swellings of the Tinaja Hills. They knew they were taking chances as they glided along through the wind-thinned moonlight, furtive shadows amid a weird company of dancing shadows that, unlike the purposeful pair, remained straining futilely at tree or crag or grotesque cactus.

Walt and Tom were after blue grouse. Once back in the hills, they had little fear of being molested by Don Sebastian's vaqueros. Getting there was the trouble. Although it was undoubtedly safer to work into the hills outside the wire and then enter the confines of the ranch, it was also much more difficult. Walt and Tom preferred to take their chances and steal northward along the western rim of Devil Canyon, comparatively easy going, rather than tackle the cliffs and crumbly, precipitous slopes west of the Regal fence. Doubtless the danger entailed had something to do with the choice of the adventuresome cowboys. Anyhow, Tom and Walt chuckled as they slipped from one clump of shadow to another, their elation growing as they drew nearer and near the lower slopes. They were close to the lip of the sinister gorge with its murmur of water rising from the black depths shut in by its overhanging walls, and several miles east of the fence.

So far as was known, nobody had ever entered Devil Canyon, and there was small prospect of anybody not completely *loco* doing so. There were legends, true, of certain prospectors who had let themselves down by ropes, and who had never reappeared; but there was no authentic proof that the stories were other than line cabin tales manufactured out of whole cloth to while away tedious winter evenings. There was no reason for prospectors or anybody else to enter Devil Canyon. It had been pretty conclusively proven that there were no mineral deposits in the Tinaja Hills, and therefore scant chance of anybody trying to explore the gloomy box canyon, the walls of which could not be climbed and the floor a tangled choke of wild growth through which could be seen, on sunny days, the black gleam of rock and the occasional glimmer of swift water. Where the Hardy boys skulked along its rim, no great distance from the southern end-wall of the box, the canyon was more than a hundred feet in depth. Twenty miles farther north, in the heart of the Tinajas, it was at least two thousand.

The growth thinned out and Tom and Walt, cradling their shotguns, hurried across a wide patch of brilliant moonlight. The wind plucked at their garments and whistled past their ears. Then, with heart-thumping unexpectedness, something else whistled past their ears!

Tom and Walt heard that screeching whistle before they heard the clanging, metallic *Cr-r-r-rack!* that whanged back and forth among the crags and tree trunks.

"Scoot!" barked the elder brother, "the blankety-blanks've spotted us!"

Tom Hardy obeyed orders and "scooted," head bent low, doubling his lean body and hugging the ground. He was rather enjoying himself: the hill slopes were close with their network of draws and dry washes and gulleys. The *vaqueros* wouldn't have much chance of running them down once they reached that inhospitable sanctuary. Horses were no good there, and Tom knew the Mexican punchers had small liking for traveling on foot. They would halt at the foot of the craggy slopes and yell profanity in two languages, bang away with their rifles, taking good care to shoot well above the heads of the fugitives, and then ride back, doubtless chuckling to themselves and hoping for better luck next time. It had happened before, just that way. Tom also chuckled, ducking instinctively as a slug yelled past rather too close for comfort. He heard another one—

"*Cr-r-rrack!* Thud."

That last was a soft, sickening sound. Tom Hardy's spine crinkled as he heard it. Almost instantly he heard also a queer little coughing sound, then a scuttering among the loose stones behind him. He skidded to a stop, whirled and stared with unbelieving eyes at the sprawled form of his brother Walt.

Heedless of the bullets that were screeching through the air or kicking up spurts of dust at his very feet, Tom Hardy raced back and knelt beside his brother's silent form. One glance was enough. There was a small blue hole in the back of Walt's neck, and the white front of his throat was ripped out by the passage of the bone-flattened slug. Walt was dead before he hit the ground.

Cursing insanely, Tom Hardy reeled to his feet, clutching his shotgun. A bullet burned a red smear along his cheek. Another ripped his coat sleeve. He flung up the shotgun, but even as the butt pressed his shoulder, common sense came to his rescue. He could not hope to damage with his futile weapon the horsemen racing toward him. Both he and Walt had left their sixguns at home, not wanting to be bothered by the weight.

"Me gettin' killed won't do Walt any good, and won't be gettin' even with them hyderphobia skunks," he muttered as he whirled and dived for the shelter of the undergrowth. The pursuit was almost upon him. His red anger was cooling to a hard vindictiveness, an icy resolve for vengeance. Swiftly he ran, ducking and dodging. Behind him crashed the pursuit. Bullets whined past.

Tom Hardy went down, end over end like a plugged rabbit. He scrambled to his feet, dazed and bleeding. A bullet had furrowed its way along the side of his head. It was little more than a scratch, but the shock had caused him to stumble and the fall had been a hard one. Into the shelter of the underbrush he reeled, triumphant yells sounding in his ears. He ducked his head low and ran madly, tearing through the growth, blood and sweat filling his eyes, blinding them. He did not see the black gulf yawning at his feet as he crashed through a final fringe of growth. With a scream of terror and despair he plunged over the lip of the canyon. Up from the black depths drifted his thinning yell, which was knifed off short. An instant later there drifted up the sound of a sullen splash, then only the worry and moan of the hurrying water.

Lean, stealthy shapes slipped through the growth. The pursuit had heard Tom Hardy's despairing yell and had guessed its meaning. They were taking no chances, however, and minutes elapsed before they crouched amid the broken bushes where the cowboy had plunged over the canyon lip. To expert eyes the story was easy to read; there was no doubt but that Tom Hardy had gone to his doom.

The searchers muttered together, faded away from the canyon lip. A few minutes later the body of Walt Hardy was dragged through the brush and thrust over the edge. Again sounded that far-off, conclusive splash. The affrighted moon hid herself behind a veil of cloud. The star eyes seemed to dim with unshed tears. Through the deepening shadow sounded the diminishing click of departing hoofs. In the black maw of the canyon, the unseen water moaned a dirge.

On the crest of a low ridge the sinister band paused. The leader, tall, broad of shoulder, face muffled by high-drawn *serape* and with but a dark glint of eyes showing beneath the brim of his wide *sombrero*, gazed steadily south by east, toward where a wounded man lay in the little cabin of Manuel Cardenas in the river village. For a moment he seemed to hesitate, glancing at the sky already streaked with the wan light of a gray dawn. He spoke tersely in Spanish:

"Too late; and tonight we have other things to do. Two nights from tonight, after midnight, will be the time. Ortego, see that all things are prepared as I instructed. *Adelante!*"

Wheeling sharply, the band drummed into the north, toward the glooming shadow of the Tinaja Hills.

CHAPTER IV

Still weak, but gaining strength rapidly, Jim Hatfield sat on the edge of his bunk in the ground floor room of Manuel Cardenas' cabin. Rosa eyed the proceedings with misgiving and disapproval. Her liquid tones voiced protest as Hatfield slowly got to his feet. The Ranger smiled down at her anxious face.

"I'll be all right, *cara mia*," he told her. "Just going to the door and back for the first time. I want to see how steady I am."

He was surprisingly "steady" for a man who had been so near death. His wound, however, once the skillful hand of Tsiang set the matter aright, had healed quickly, with no bad after effects. Rosa's skillful nursing was the only added touch needed. Hatfield could feel strength surging back into his veins by the hour. Reaching the door, he stood with one hand on the jamb, gazing into the sun-washed plaza. His eyes narrowed slightly as he observed, a little distance from the cabin, two easily lounging figures, heavy rifles resting in crooked arms. Dark faces split into pleased grins as the watchers observed him; they waved their hands in friendly fashion. Hatfield waved back and turned to Rosa.

"Who are they and what're they doing here?" he asked.

Rosa shrugged with Latin eloquence.

"They watch," she replied tersely. "One takes no chances with *los caballeros de la noche*. Who knows but they might choose to ride this way again? Six of their number died by your hand, *Capitan*, and they must know that you still live and are here. So our young men watch, day and night. You have made our young men brave, *Capitan*. Let the riders of the night come, if they dare. We no longer fear them."

Hatfield nodded his understanding and appreciation.

"Your dad ought to be getting back soon," he remarked.

Rosa crossed the cabin to an inner room and gazed from a window that faced the west.

"Even now two riders come this way," she said when she returned to the large room.

"That ought to be he and Captain Bill," Hatfield replied eagerly.

Rosa's gentle hand touched his arm. "Rest, *Capitan*," she urged. "Not yet are you wholly strong."

"I could lift a horse," Hatfield grinned in reply. Nevertheless, he permitted her to lead him back to the couch. He was sitting propped up with pillows when the hoofs sounded without. A moment later Manuel Cardenas entered, accompanied by a tall old man with frosty blue eyes and a grizzled moustache. The eyes lighted with pleased relief as they rested on Hatfield's face.

"Well, loafin' as usual, I see," he grunted.

Hatfield grinned and they shook hands warmly.

"Now tell me all about it," ordered Captain McDowell.

Hatfield proceeded to do so. The old Ranger leader listened in silence, pulling at his moustache. His eyes were very cold by the time Hatfield finished.

"I want to stick around till I get to the bottom of this, sir," the Lone Wolf concluded.

"I know how you feel about it," Captain Bill agreed, "and that gang needs rounding up. They can't get away with this business of shooting down Rangers in performance of their duty. Yeah, you can stay on the job here, Jim, though we need you bad enough other places, what with the trouble up in the Panhandle and around Cero Diable and such. Not a man to spare, much less the troop everybody over in this district is yelling for. Round 'em up, Jim!"

Hatfield said nothing, but as McDowell gazed at his

stern face, he was reminded of something he had seen in an Indian village, many years before:

A captured eagle was fettered to its perch, while in the trees surrounding the open space, a flock of ribald crows jeered and cursed at the restrained king of the heavens. The eagle made no outcry, only stared with fierce, brooding eyes, mantling itself from time to time.

Bill McDowell was in some ways a strange man. Sitting his horse, he stared at the lordly bird. Suddenly he spun a coin to the Indian who owned it, leaned from the saddle and with one sweep of his knife cut the cord that held the eagle captive.

"Go after that scum, big feller!" he shouted, giving the freed bird a push.

With a rush like a mighty wind, the great wings unfolded and the huge bird took the air. One fierce, wild scream it gave: and the air was fillled with whizzing black shapes that yelled their terror and went away from there so fast they smoked.

"And that's what'll happen when he gets on his feet again," Captain Bill chuckled as the recalled incident faded and the lean, bronzed face of his ace Ranger appeared before his eyes once more.

"What's that, sir?" Hatfield asked.

"Nothing," Cap. Bill chuckled. "I was just gonna say that in addition to rounding up this night ridin' gang, I want you to take a look at this range war what's threatening to bust between Devil Anse McCoy's Bar M outfit and Don Sebastian Gomez's Regal ranch. There has been trouble between the outfits before and yelps for a Ranger troop to cool it down. Now to make matters worse, two of McCoy's riders went sneaking through Gomez's wire night before last to hunt grouse and haven't showed up since. McCoy swears Gomez has done something to 'em and is for riding over and cleaning out the Regal. You've heard of McCoy—he's liable to be as good as his word."

Hatfield nodded. "Just who is Gomez?" he asked. "I don't seem to remember anything particular about him."

"Spanish blood, Mexican born," McDowell replied. "Come up here and bought the ranch from old man Turner, ten years back. Got into a row with McCoy and fenced his spread. Pretty well off, I think. Hear he owns some property down in Mexico—and a mine or two."

"Owns mines?"

"So I hear. They won't pay over much, though. Mexican owned mines are usually worked shiftlessly."

Hatfield nodded, his eyes cold and speculative.

"Owns mines," he repeated, "and a Mexican."

"Yes," said Captain Bill. "Well, Jim, I'm going to ride on over east. Manuel tells me the doc here says you'll be up and kickin' before very long, now that the bullet's out. That Chinaman sure must know his business! The doc told Manuel the slug was lying right 'longside your heart, and pressing 'gainst the aorta, the big trunk artery which carries the blood from the heart. He said it was just a matter of time before friction would have caused the artery to burst, and that would have been the end of you. He said, the way that bullet was placed, he'd swear on a stack of Bibles it wouldn't be possible to take it out without killing you."

Hatfield nodded gravely. "I want to see that Chinese doctor and thank him," he replied. "Manuel tells me he rode off after performing the operation; said all I'd need after that was good nursing and that Rosa could be relied on to provide that. She has been doing a swell job of it, too," he added, glancing gratefully at the dark-eyed Mexican girl, who flushed with pleasure and bowed her shapely head.

After Captain Bill had ridden away, Hatfield called the old Mexican to him.

"Manuel," he said, "I'm going to move upstairs to my old room now. I've kept you out of your bed long enough. It'll make things more convenient for you and Rosa."

"But, *Capitan,* you should not climb stairs; you are not strong," protested Manuel.

"I need exercise to get my strength back," Hatfield

pointed out. "Besides," he added, using an argument that he knew would appeal, "it'll be quieter up there. I won't hear you getting up to go to work and I'll sleep more."

Manuel was still dubious, but he finally gave doubtful assent.

It was quiet in the little room under the eaves and Hatfield went to sleep early. He slept soundly while the great clock in the sky wheeled westward and the hour of midnight came and went. He was still sleeping as two shadowy figures slid furtively from the conceal-ment of a grove and approached the cabin. Like mist wraiths they moved, but purposefully and with the sureness of men who have previously looked over the ground and are thoroughly familiar with it. From the gloom beneath a tree they surveyed the two guards who sat on either side of the door, nodding over their rifles. Carefully avoiding the door, they approached the cabin from the side. A moment later they crouched beneath a window and stared into a dimly lighted room. Almost within arm's reach was a couch upon which lay a long figure breathing steadily in sleep.

One of the crouching shadows bore a strangely shaped bundle, which he handled with the greatest care. Gingerly he drew something from beneath the covering, his fingers clamping it with apprehensive firm-ness. His companion shrank back, and cursed softly as a loose stone clicked sharply underfoot. The other raised his arm in a throwing gesture. A moment later the two faded swiftly around a corner of the cabin and vanished toward the north.

Jim Hatfield slept soundly, but he slept with the hair-trigger lightness of a man whose blanket companion has for years been constant danger. Suddenly he snapped wide awake and lay tensely alert, every sense working overtime. In his ears still rang the echo of a slight clicking sound. For a quivering moment he heard nothing; then up the open stairway from the large room on the ground floor drifted an almost inaudible swishing thud followed by a startled grunt and a strange dry buzzing. Then utter silence, but a silence acrawl with nameless dread.

Noiselessly Hatfield dropped his feet to the floor and sat up, wrapping the heavy robe he wore about him. He slipped his feet into soft-soled Mexican sandals that lay nearby, drew one of his heavy guns from his holster, and glided to the head of the stairs. He knelt and peered into the room below. For a quivering instant he stared at what he saw by the uncertain light of a single small oil lamp, and the hand that gripped the big gun grew moist of palm with a cold sweat.

Close to the open window was the couch on which Hatfield himself had slept the night before and many nights previous. Old Manuel Cardenas lay there now, lay rigid as a cataleptic, eyes wide and staring, his very breath caught motionless in his swelling throat. And on his breast, sinewy coils looped in a loose fold, evil head reared up and back, was a huge rattlesnake; not the little sidewinder of the desert, but one of the terrible monsters of the hills—six feet of awful death.

Red with rage were the snake's baleful eyes and from the raised fangs dripped venom like brown ink. Straight into those terrible fiery eyes stared old Manuel Cardenas, knowing well that no move of his could hope to beat the flashing death stroke of the rattler, knowing that the slightest flicker of a muscle or quiver of an eyelid would bring those needle fangs slashing at his face.

Hatfield knew it too, and knew that human endurance could not hold that stricken pose for long. Any instant strained muscles, crying aloud for relief, would flex in involuntary movement and arouse the already maddened snake to instant and deadly action.

Forward jutted the big gun, but the hand ordinarily so rock-steady trembled. Sweat bursting out on his face, the Ranger fought to control the weakness due to the terrible draining of blood he had undergone. The shooting angle was bad and the light dim and uncertain.

"If I miss, I'll drill Manuel!" he panted through dry lips, "but the snake will get him, anyhow!"

The snake's muscles swelled, its grim head poised for the forward stroke. With a terrible effort of the will, Hatfield tensed his trembling hand, his slim finger squeezed the trigger.

The roar of the gun was echoed by Manuel's scream of terror. Hatfield bounded down the stairs as the old Mexican thudded to the floor beside his couch.

And on the far side of the couch, writhing, thrashing, lay the body of the rattlesnake, its head smashed to fragments by the heavy bullet.

"Did it strike you?" shouted Hatfield.

"No!" gasped Manuel. "Sangre de Cristo! What—"

Hatfield bounded to the door, flung it open and met the babbling sentinels, now thoroughly wide awake.

" 'Round to the other side!" he shouted, and led the way.

They reached the side of the cabin which fronted on the north, and as they whisked around the corner, the click of distant hoofs sounded. From out a grove two mounted figures fled through the pale moonlight.

Hatfield snatched a rifle from one of the guards, clamped the butt to his shoulder. His level gray eyes glanced along the sights.

The rifle roared, yellowish flame flickered from its muzzle, and a spurt of smoke.

Staring through the thinning smoke cloud, Hatfield saw one of the speeding horses go down in a sprawling heap. The rider was hurled over its head but lit on his feet, stumbled, staggered, caught his balance. His companion jerked his mount to a rearing halt and the other bounded forward and leaped to the horse's back behind the saddle.

Up came the heavy rifle. Once more the steady eyes glanced along the sights. But at that instant a film of cloud drifted across the face of the moon. Hatfield pulled trigger, but knew he had missed. By the time the moon was clear again, a clump of trees hid the horse and its double load from view.

Walking unsteadily, Hatfield made his way to the fallen horse. It was stone dead when he reached it. There was nothing about the plain and serviceable rig that might serve to identify the rider. It was a branded horse, however, the brand easy to read—Lazy R!

Leaning heavily on Manuel Cardenas' arm, Hatfield made his way back to the cabin. He was feeling very weak and shaky. Old Manuel was pouring forth thanks and wondering questions.

"Threw the rattler through the window," Hatfield told him. "They must have sneaked up when the guards weren't looking or were dozing. Fine notions that outfit's got!"

A light dawned on the old Mexican. "Capitan," he gasped, "each night before, you have slept on that couch! They knew! Capitan, they made the mistake! They thought it was you!"

"Seems probable," Hatfield admitted.

Most of the village was thronged about the cabin, including the old doctor. He bundled Hatfield into bed with scant ceremony, anxiously examined his newly healed wound and carefully looked him over in general. Finally he sighed with relief.

"No great harm appears to be done," he said. "Only, I fear, señor, that this night's work will mean a considerable length of time added to your period of confinement here. You are fortunate that your wound did not break afresh."

Hatfield nodded, feeling too sick and weary for comment. He raised himself on a shaky elbow, however, and asked old Manuel a question—

"What outfit hereabouts has a Lazy R for its branding mark?"

Manuel Cardenas hesitated, and replied with evident reluctance:

"That, Capitan, is the brand of the Regal ranch, owned by Don Sebastian Gomez."

Chapter V

When the Hardy boys did not return from their hunting trip there was trouble brewing. Both rode for old Anse McCoy's Bar M. Their fellow workers knew their intentions when they left the bunkhouse, shotguns under their arms. Blaine Hatch, the Bar M foreman, went up to the big gray ranchhouse to see old Anse about it when Tom and Walt had been absent a day and two nights.

"Somethin's happened," he told the Bar M owner. "Them fellers didn't callate on nestin' up in them hills. They'd oughta been back yest'day aft'noon. They've either got theirselves hurted some way or—"

Hatch, a man of conservative speech, hesitated to finish the sentence. Vicious old Anse finished it for him.

"Or else that greaser has done 'way with 'em!" the ranch owner snarled, his black eyes, brilliant as those of a snake despite his years, blazing from under his white tufts of brows. With his beak of a nose, his tightly clamped lips and his lean, jutting jaw, he reminded Blaine Hatch of some fierce old bird of prey.

"I don't hardly callate Gomez'd do anythin' like that," the foreman endeavored to temporize, "mebbe they—"

"Mebbe!" blared old Anse. "Yuh mark my word, Blaine, yuh ain't never gonna see Tom or Walt alive agin. You'll find their corpses over there in the brush somewheres. Git the boys t'gether and go look for 'em. Move, blankety-blank-blank yuh!"

Blaine Hatch "moved." At the head of his grimfaced

33

waddies he rode to the tall iron gates that barred the road leading to the Lazy R ranchhouse.

"They've seen us," remarked Hatch, gesturing to the Lazy R vaqueros lounging just inside the gates, rifles cradled in their arms.

"To hell with 'em!" snarled Chet Madison, a heavy-faced cowboy with a stubby beard and snappy little eyes. Chet was belligerent of disposition and often came to words with the conservative Hatch. It was understood that he was in line for the foremanship should Hatch happen to quit.

Blaine Hatch bluntly stated the reasons for the visit and demanded permission to search the Regal range for the missing punchers. A wordy wrangle ensued and Don Sebastian was sent for.

Straight as a lance was Don Sebastian Gomez, despite the years that had sprinkled his thick black hair with gray. His eyes were very dark, but his skin, under the deep bronze of Texas wind and Texas sun, was singularly light. Pride sat on his lean face and showed in his stately bearing, the scorching, arrogant, and ofttimes ruthless pride of generations born to rule.

Don Sebastian at first refused the desired permission, and the two forces faced each other tensely across the wire. Then his foreman, Pedro Zorrila, a lean dark Mexican with a face terribly seamed and distorted by scars, whispered in his employer's ear, cocking an eye toward the lowering sky, across which dark masses of cloud were scudding before a wailing wind. Don Sebastian finally nodded reluctantly, turned on his heel and returned to the ranchhouse. The saturnine foreman unlocked the big gates and swung them wide.

"Enter, señors," he invited, grinning derisively.

"Now what does Pizen Pete Zorrila find so funny?" growled Chet Madison as they clicked across the range.

He understood, or thought he did, a little later, when the wind increased to a shrieking bellow and the rain came down in sheets, effectually washing away any possible traces of the fate of the two missing cowboys.

"Outsmarted us!" cursed Chet Madison. "The scar-faced foreman saw this rain was comin'. He knowed it'd wipe out any tracks or anythin'. C'mon, let's cut 'round the lower box end of Devil Canyon and see if we can pick up their trail where they come through the wire. I know 'bout where they was callatin' to cut through."

They picked up nothing, either there or deep in the hills. Late the following afternoon they rode back along the rim of Devil Canyon.

"Did for 'em and flang 'em inter that damn hole, I bet my last peso!" snarled Chet Madison. "With that river down there what comes out under the box wall and goes scootin' inter the hills at a mile a minute, the bodies would be carried off where nobody could find 'em. Yeah, that's what happened, and yuh can lay to it!"

"Mebbe we'll find the boys safe to home when we get back to the ranch," Hatch remarked hopefully.

"Yeah!" snorted Chet Madison, "mebbe!"

Pedro Zorrila, still smiling his mocking smile, let them out the locked gate. Chet Madison regarded him gloomily.

"I'll be seein' you, feller!" he promised with venomous emphasis.

"Si!" the Mexican replied softly. "Look closely, señor!"

The Hardy brothers were not at the ranch when the weary searchers rode in. Old Anse McCoy raved curses and vowed dire vengeance on Don Sebastian and all his tribe. Dent Crane, the sheriff of the county, heard of what had happened and rode out to the Bar M. He finally extracted a grudging promise from old Anse not to do anything reckless while he had no positive proof of anybody's guilt. The fate of the two cowboys remained shrouded in mystery. Months passed and time dimmed the dangerous edge of the happening.

And then—*Tom Hardy came back!*

Nobody recognized him at first when he crawled into the Bar M bunkhouse in the gray light of a rainy morning. One eye was gone and he was all but blind in the one remaining. He was toothless, almost hairless. His hands were crooked claws, blotched with horrible mottlings that were as new burns. One arm was twisted, shrunken, and useless. It was as if the very bones had turned to limp jelly under the withered flesh. His mouth was a festering sore from which wheezed croaking words that held no meaning.

Old Anse McCoy, hearing the uproar, pulled on a few clothes and hobbled to the bunkhouse. Tom Hardy was rattling in his ravaged throat. He had evidently used the last atom of life spark to drag his seared and blasted body to the Bar M ranch.

Old Anse, rasping curses, knelt beside Chet Madison and Blaine Hatch. His straining ears caught ragged words—

"Man—no face—devil—devil—" gurgled the dying cowboy. His heaving chest swelled with mighty effort. He gagged, choked, champed his toothless jaws.

"No face!" he repeated in a thin shriek. Another spasm of effort. Then, just as the writhing soul tore itself free from the tortured body—

"I—I—tell—I—Gomez—Gomez!"

The arching chest sank, seemed to cave in. The mangled face twisted grotesquely, relaxed. Tom Hardy rattled once more in his throat, exhaled a last whistling breath, and lay silent and motionless, his one bleared eye fixed and glazing.

Chet Madison rose to his feet, face set like stone. Old Anse was raving curses.

"What did they do to him?" demanded a cowboy in an awed voice.

Chet Madison stared at the pitifully scarred face, and the livid distorted hands.

"Burnt him or poured acid or somethin' on him," Madison declared. "Yeah, that's it—acid! Acid does things like that to a feller. That's a greaser trick for yuh!"

A sound like the worrying note of a pack of wolves swept through the bunkhouse. Eyes glared, hands balled into iron-hard fists.

"What'd he mean 'bout 'no face'?" somebody wondered.

"He ain't got none left, has he?" was pointed out.

The questioner shook his head. "Don't callate he was talkin' 'bout hisself—didn't sound that way."

"That chopped up foreman, Pizen Pete Zorrila, ain't got much face left either," remarked a grizzled old puncher. "I heerd tell the Yaquis caught him oncet and worked on him with their knives. He shore looks it."

"Looks like a Yaqui hisself to me," another commented. "And this"—pointing to dead Tom Hardy—"looks like Yaqui work!"

"We'll find out!" Old Anse promised grimly, "and when we do! All right, you fellers, t'day's payday. Yuh might as well come on up to the house and get it right now. When yuh ride to town, Blaine, see the sheriff and the coroner and make 'rangements with the undertaker to plant pore Tom."

Seething with anger, wrangling among themselves, the Bar M punchers rode to town.

Vegas was more than an ordinary cow town. Half a dozen trails centered there, two of them the shortest and most direct route to Mexico, which was considered an advantage by a number of gentlemen who spent much of their time in the Tinaja Hills, who made their money in questionable ways, and came to Vegas to enjoy it. Cowboys from ranches within a fifty mile radius also came to Vegas. Trail herds passed that way and the riders who accompanied them stopped on their way back, pockets filled, time on their hands. Just south of the Rio Grande, and less than a score of miles distant, were a number of productive mines, mostly American owned and worked. The brawny muckers and hardrock men also found Vegas attractive. Gamblers and dancehall girls came along to reap the harvest always ripe in a roarin' cattle and mining town. Saloon keepers, plenty of them, had, apparently, always been there.

The resulting mixture was as lively a devil's brew as could be desired by the most fastidious. Particularly so on paydays. The mines and most of the ranches, by a singular coincidence, arranged to have paydays fall on identical dates. Which did not tend to lessen the activities.

The Bar M boys hit town, still wrangling. Several were for riding direct to the Lazy R and having it out with the Gomez outfit. More rational spirits, Blaine Hatch in particular, counseled against such precipitate action. Finally, even the most belligerent succumbed to the seductive lure of Hogface Holliday's First Chance saloon.

And then fate or, more likely, the sardonic gods of the Tinaja Hills, took a hand. The Bar M outfit and a dozen of Don Sebastian's vaqueros, approaching from opposite directions, arrived before the First Chance at the same instant.

"Yuh murderin', saddle-colored, snake-eyed blankety-blanks!" howled a Bar M puncher.

For a tense instant after that hate-charged yell there was dead silence, broken only by the champing of the horses and the castenating of their impatient hoofs. The entire neighborhood, sensing grim tragedy in the making, seemed to hold its breath. Then the street fairly exploded with the roar of sixshooters.

Outnumbered almost two to one, the vaqueros broke first, racing their horses out of town, flinging lead over their shoulders. Three didn't ride. They lay sprawled grotesquely in the dust of the street.

Blaine Hatch also lay in the dust, silent and very still. Beside him lay the youngest Bar M cowboy, a blue hole between his staring eyes.

The Lazy R became an armed camp. The Bar M another. Chet Madison, now foreman, conferred with old Anse McCoy and planned a night raid. Sheriff Dent Crane swore in a number of special deputies and warned both factions to keep the peace. Old Anse told him flatly to go to hell. Don Sebastian Gomez, with chill courtesy, declined to call in his armed patrols. Sheriff Crane had little hope of anything like a peaceful settlement.

"A range war is gonna bust sooner or later," he pessimistically declared to his chief deputy, Highpockets Hilton. Highpockets agreed with enthusiasm, and cleaned his rifle.

Word came that Nelson Page, who had purchased the big Cross P which lay to the south and west of the Bar M, had telegraphed the governor for a troop of Texas Rangers.

"I shore hope he gets them," said Sheriff Crane, "but with things like they is along the Border over east and up in the Panhandle, to say nothin' of the trouble over in the oil fields, I ain't got much hopes. 'Case for local 'thorities' is the answer he'll get. Yuh see if he don't."

"Page ain't been in this country over long," remarked Highpockets.

"Nope, come from over East coupla years ago, Eastern feller what usta live in the West. Come out here and bought the old Turner place. Nobody sees much of him. Nice feller, though, ev'body says."

A tense week followed. A second began. Shots were exchanged across the line fence by Lazy R vaqueros and Bar M punchers.

Don Sebastian Gomez rode to the sheriff's office.

"I desire to report that three of my men have been missing for four days," he told Dent Crane. "I do not expect them to be found alive, but I wish you would institute a search for their bodies, so that they can be given decent burial."

Sheriff Crane swore wearily after the hidalgo had departed.

"What's the matter with you?" he demanded as Highpockets Hilton entered the office, shaking his head, clucking behind his teeth.

Highpockets removed his hat and wiped his damp forehead. "I need a drink!" he announced. "I done seed the goshawfulest thing, Dent. Three Mexicans brought a Injun lookin' feller inter Doc Austin's office; feller was nigh dead—couldn't more'n mumble. He was all covered with big sores and places like he'd been rubbed by a redhot iron. Doc started workin' on him, but he cashed in 'most 'fore Doc'd hardly begun. I was busy handin' Doc things and when him and me turned 'round to ask the Mexicans what had happened to the feller, they'd done snuk out. I couldn't find hide or hair of any of 'em."

Highpockets glanced nervously around and lowered his voice.

"Dent," he said, "that feller looked like he'd had jest the same kind of goin' over as what pore Tom Hardy got. I tell yuh there's somethin' almighty wrong in this deestrict. There's a prize gang holin' up 'round hereabouts, and I ain't meanin' mebbe."

"All the muy malo hombres from both sides the Line 'pears to be headin' this way," growled the sheriff.

"Yeah, I jest noticed a prize spec'men ride up to Hogface Holliday's saloon—a big tall jigger forkin' the plumb finest golden sorrel hoss yuh ever laid eyes on, the kind of cayuse yuh dream 'bout but don't see."

"Range tramp, eh?" grunted the sheriff. Highpockets shook his head.

"Nope, not a puncher—leastwise he didn't wear cowhands' outfittin'. Gambler, I'd say—black hat and coat, white shirt, black necktie. Sorta sunburned for a gambler, but he had the hands, long and slimlike. Funny eyes. Shiny gray, and long. I was jest comin' outa the Fust Chance when he unforked, and he looked at me— the sorta look what goes right on inside yuh and sees whether yore liver is white or reg'lation color and if they's any yaller streakin's 'longside yore backbone. It was jest a kinda passin'-over look, but if that big jigger ever looked at me and meant it, I'd go 'way from there so fast yuh could hear me whiz ten minutes after passin' a given p'int!"

Sheriff Crane, recalling the notches Highpockets would be justified in cutting on the butt of his old single-action Colt, if he were the kind that cut notches, was impressed.

CHAPTER VI

THINGS were lively in the First Chance saloon. The returning riders from several big trail herds were in town. A holiday was being observed at the mines below the Line and the miners had come to town in force. The threatened range war was an added attraction, and ranch owners and riders were endeavoring not to miss anything. Saloon, dancehall, gambling hall and other places, the least said about the better, prospered accordingly. Hogface Holliday's First Chance was the biggest and showiest place in Vegas. It attracted the best heeled crowd, and the saltiest. Hogface was reputed to run straight games. His girls, mostly sloe-eyed señoritas, were pretty and good dancers. Hogface sold the best whisky he could obtain, and charged plenty for it. Hogface himself was shaped like one of his own whisky barrels, and some folks said he was just as full of poison, although the general agreement was that Hogface was a square shooter. He had amazingly long arms, his great hairy hands hanging almost to his knees; thick, bowed legs; a mighty spread of shoulder; and a neck as thick and corded as the trunk of a fir tree. His eyes were small and twinkly, set deep in creases of grin-wrinkled fat, his jaw massive, his nose short and tip-tilted. A glorious mane of crinkly, iron-gray hair swept back from his big, dome-shaped forehead. He looked slow and awkward, but he could jump the high bar from a flat-footed start and hit with both hands while still in the air. Gentlemen with belligerent dispositions, fooled by his fatty appearance and apparent slowness, had been know to pick fights with Hogface—one to a man!

"This *pueblo* is gonna howl 'fore come mawnin',"

41

Hogface's head bartender remarked, mopping his per-
spiring face with a bar towel. "Here it ain't much past
the middle of the afternoon and I been pourin' whisky
so fast the bar's smokin'."

Hogface nodded absently; he was watching a poker
table on the far side of the room, a table where high
stakes prevailed. All the tables were busy, the roulette
wheel was spinning cheerily, there was a click and
rattle from the direction of the crap table, and the
orchestra was already tuning up.

The particular table that held Hogface's attention
was occupied by five men. Three Hogface knew to be
cowmen, owners of small ranches. A fourth was a
saturnine individual with a swarthy complexion, small,
intensely black eyes that burned brightly, a thin gash
of a mouth with too red lips, and a crooked nose. He
was tall, lean, and sinewy with supple hands that were
never still. Hogface's glance passed over him with scant
approval and rested on the fifth man, and remained
there, speculative, appraising.

"Now where did he come from?" he grunted under
his breath. "Looks like a plum salty jigger and handles
cyards like he shore knows somethin' 'bout 'em."

He pondered the man's costume—long black coat,
extremely well fitting, fine corduroy breeches, dark in
color, stuffed into shiny boots, wine-colored vest, snowy
white shirt and black string tie. He wore a broad-
brimmed black hat pulled low over his eyes. Hogface
did not miss the heavy double cartridge belts that
snugged about his lean waist.

"Gambler's get-up, all right," nodded the saloonkeeper, "and them hands look like gambler's hands, too.
Gosh! he's a tall feller! And look at them shoulders!
Funny lookin' eyes, too—sorta the color of a waterfall on
a frosty mawnin'. Callate they don't miss much. Well,
he'll need to keep 'em open with Nigger Mike Brocas
settin' 'crost the table from him!"

His gaze shifted to the swarthy man and the twinkle
in his little eyes turned grim and menacing.

"If Anse McCoy didn't set sich store by that half-breed, I'd kicked him outa here long time back," he growled. "Trouble jest nacherly rises up and is wherever that snake-eyed coot happens to be!"

For some time he watched Nigger Mike's play, but finally gave it up with a disgusted growl—

"Crooked as hell or I'm a sheepherder, but nobody's ever been able to ketch him at it. If I ever do—!"

Nigger Mike Brocas worked for Anse McCoy, when he was not gambling. He was a tophand with horse, rope, branding iron, knife or gun, and was reputed to be the best tracker west of the Pecos. His reputation as a poker player was high, and slightly fuzzy around the edges, although nobody had ever been able actually to pin anything crooked on him. Perhaps the fact that the supple hands, so lightning fast with cards, were equally fast with the heavy Smith & Wesson he wore far to the front on the left side of his belt had something to do with it. Brocas was a cross-pull man, a master of that uncommon but deadly draw.

"Fastest man on the draw in the hull blankety-blank state of Texas," old Anse was wont to say. Folks who had seen Nigger Mike in action did not take exception to the statement.

Nigger Mike did not mix much with the other Bar M hands. He preferred solitude, as a rule, and got it. His nickname was due to his coloring, not to blood. Nigger Mike was an Apache, with a dash of bad white. He had all the vices of both races, and none of the virtues. It pleased old Anse's general devilishness of disposition to keep the saddle-colored hellion around, and the Bar M riders, clannish to a degree, stood by him as a matter of course.

As Hogface Holliday stood watching the stud poker game in the corner of his saloon, two people were riding toward Vegas from opposite directions. One was a girl, the other a man. The man pulled up in front of a livery stable and left his tall black horse in the care of the liveryman, asked a question or two, and headed purposefully up Lucky Nugget Street in the direction of the First Chance saloon, gazing about him with the interest of one who surveys unfamiliar scenes. The girl, arriving in town a little later, tied her sturdy pinto to a rack, and nodding from time to time to acquaintances, sauntered down Lucky Nugget Street glancing into shop windows, pausing before those with marked feminine appeal, entering now and then and making occasional purchases. Everywhere she was greeted with smiles and nods, all extremely respectful in manner. She was still some distance from the Last Chance saloon when the row broke. The man approaching from the opposite direction was much nearer Hogface's place.

The game at the table in the corner was a quiet one, as games for large stakes usually are. Nothing was to be heard save the soft slither of the cards, the click of chips and occasional monosyllables from one or other of the players. Bets were shoved forward and pots gathered in without comment, as a rule.

Two of the cowmen were winning, one was losing. The tall stranger in the black coat was holding his own. His play was quiet and courteous and the eyes of the three ranchers rested on him from time to time with evident approval. "Gambler by perfession, mebbe," was their inward comment, "but a squareshooter and a plumb gent."

There was nothing of approval in Nigger Mike Brocas' black glare, however. Stud poker is a peculiar and at times intensely irritating game. One player may be losing steadily or barely holding his own, and still he may be the very man who is walloping the living blue blazing daylights out of some other luckless individual. Which does not endear him to the individual in question, despite the fact that he is steadily passing his winnings on to others in the game.

Such was the situation that had developed in Hogface Holliday's place. Nigger Mike was losing steadily, and the tall stranger was to blame. Pot after pot he took from Mike, pots that hurt to lose. Then, slowly but steadily, he would dribble away his winnings to the two affluent cowmen until he was barely even with the game. Nigger Mike ground his stubby teeth, writhed his thin lips and glared. The tall stranger paid scant attention to his fury. Only once, when Nigger Mike muttered something under his breath, he turned the level gaze of his gray eyes full on the half-breed's face. Nigger Mike met that bleak stare for an instant, then shifted his own burning black eyes uneasily. Much of the truculence left those eyes, but it was replaced by a sly craftiness of expression that those familiar with him would have counted more dangerous than his glares. The tall stranger apparently took no notice of Mike's change of expression. The half-breed indulged in a satisfied smirk that fleeted across his dark countenance like the shadow of a buzzard's wing across a stagnant pool.

Hogface kept watching the table, dividing his attention between it and another a little distance away. Half a dozen of the Bar M cowboys, including the heavy-faced foreman Chet Madison, wrangled amicably there over a game of seven-toed jack. Knowing the penchant of the Bar M outfit to back up its own, right or wrong, Hogface was worried about that table. His uncanny perspicacity, amounting almost to second sight, told the big saloonkeeper that trouble was brewing.

With the suddenness of a lightning flash it broke. Nigger Mike was dealing, the cards flowing from beneath his supple fingers like swift water. Each man glanced at his hole card as it fell to him. Nigger Mike raised the corner of his last, with elaborate casualness. He had a king showing. The tall stranger across the table had an ace of hearts for his up card. The hole cards of each were, of course, face downward on the table. Nigger Mike glanced up, the smirk again in his eyes; he opened his lips to speak. What he intended saying was never known.

In a flashing blur of motion, the stranger's long left arm shot across the table. Fingers like rods of nickel steel clamped the half-breed's wrist, jerking him forward. A card spun from Nigger Mike's sleeve. The tall man let go Nigger Mike's wrist and caught it while it was still in the air. At the same instant he flipped his own hole card face up: it was the ace of spades. And the torn card gripped between thumb and fingers of his left hand was also an ace of spades!

Like steel grinding on ice, the tall man's voice lashed out at the half-breed—

"Not quite fast enough, you cheat!"

Nigger Mike moved with the vicious deadliness of the sidewinder. Like the venomous, unutterably swift sideways stroke of the treacherous little snake was his cross-draw, the big Smith & Wesson leaping from its holster like a living thing. The room echoed to the crash of a shot.

Nigger Mike reeled back, the half-drawn Smith still gripped in his stiffened right hand, a look of utmost astonishment on his livid face. He hit the floor all in a heap, a rapidly spreading smudge drenching the left shoulder and breast of his gaudy silk shirt, the unfired Smith clattering across the boards. In the moment of stunned silence following, the tall stranger's soft drawl sounded clearly.

"Not quite fast enough that time, either!"

Rigid as steel he stood, the torn ace of spades still gripped in his left hand for all to see. In his right was a long black gun from whose muzzle wisped a threat of smoke.

With a roar the room came to life. Chairs crashed at the Bar M table. Chet Madison leaped to his feet, bellowing curses. Half a dozen hands snapped to holsters.

The torn card fluttered from the tall man's hand. In its place, as if by magic, was a second long Colt. Twin black muzzles yawned toward the Bar M table. The cold voice slid smoothly through the turmoil and seemed to hit Chet Madison squarely between the eyes—

"Friend of yours?"

"Blankety-blank-blank yuh!" bawled Madison, "that's a Bar M hand yuh plugged!"

The tall man's level green gaze bored Madison's snapping eyes. His voice dripped acid contempt—

"What does the Bar M outfit raise—skunks?"

For a moment it appeared Madison would have a stroke. His face turned purple, his jaw sagged, his eyes seemed to pop from his head. He tried to speak, but only a throaty gurgle came forth. It was another voice that answered the question—

"It's a man's outfit, feller, I'm here tellin' yuh!"

Chapter VII

The tall stranger had sat facing the swinging doors of the saloon. Now there was a discreetly empty lane in front of the table, extending to the door. Down this lane a man was sauntering, his gait leisurely, apparently oblivious to the surcharged atmosphere of the room. The tall stranger was perhaps the only person in the saloon who had noticed him shove the swinging doors apart and enter. And, the moment of his entrance, across the tall man's memory had fleeted a miniature he had once seen of Armand de Rance, glorious sinner, handsomest, most gifted, most magnificent man of an age of magnificent men. Here was the same cameo regularity of feature, the same blazing black eyes, the same figure that reminded one of an unsheathed sword. He was broad of shoulder, deep of chest, and of a stature far above the ordinary of men. But tall as he was, he had to lift his eyes slightly to meet the level gaze of the man who stood across the table from where Nigger Mike Brocas lay in a bleeding heap upon the floor.

"That'll be far enough."

The tall man spoke quietly, but there was that in his voice which halted the newcomer, although with nothing of fear in his look or pose. At the same instant Hogface Holliday's deep-toned roar sounded above the rising babble of sound. The old saloonkeeper was standing with his back against the bar, a cocked sawed-off shotgun clamped to his shoulder. Flanking him stood his four bartenders, likewise armed.

"We've had all the trouble we're gonna have!" boomed Hogface. "The fust jigger what makes a funny move is gonna have so many buckshot holes in his carcass he'll freeze t'death from the wind blowin' through 'em. Take yore hand off yore gun, Chet!"

Madison and the Bar M punchers obeyed, albeit reluctantly. They knew Hogface meant business and wasn't given to making idle threats.

The tall man and the newcomer still stood eyeing each other, ignoring all that was going on around them. A hush of expectancy fell over the crowd, in which the newcomer's voice rang clear—

"Sorta big skookum he-wolf, eh? Well, it ain't hard to talk salty when yuh're doin' it back of a coupla onpenned hawglegs, pertickler when yuh're speakin' to a man what don't happen to be heeled jest at the moment."

The tall man had already noticed that the handsome newcomer wore neither cartridge belt nor holster.

With a smooth, graceful movement he holstered the long Colts. A glance had assured him that Hogface and his bartenders had the situation well in hand and that there would be no promiscuous gunplay while those deadly sawed-offs were trained on the crowd. An instant later his belt and holsters thudded on the green table top. He walked around the table, glanced at Nigger Mike's unconscious form, and faced the newcomer.

"It isn't clear just what hand you are playing in this game," he said softly, "suppose you explain."

The other's gaze did not waver. "As I come in the door, I heerd yuh ask a question, that's all," he replied.

"Well, you answered it, didn't you? Have you any proof to back up that answer—proof to contradict that specimen on the floor there? That's wearing a Bar M brand, and if it doesn't belong on a skunk ranch, I don't know skunks!"

The other tensed. "Yeah," he said, his voice icily smooth, "I got proof to back up what I said when I come in. Here it is!"

The blow that followed the words was as the lashing stroke of a mountain lion's paw; but before it had traveled six inches it was blocked. At the same instant a fist like the slim, steely face of a sledgehammer smashed against the newcomer's jaw. He hit the floor with a crash that shook the building.

But he didn't stay there. He came off the boards like a bouncing rubber ball, hitting with both hands. A jabbing left got past the tall man's guard and cut his lip. A straight right sent him reeling back a pace. He covered up, weaving and ducking, a grin that was almost friendly twitching the corners of his wide mouth, and his gray eyes were sunny—the eyes of a man who is thoroughly enjoying himself. He let go a ripping uppercut and it caught the other squarely on the point of the chin. Again he hit the floor, and again he came off it with a bound, swinging both fists. The tall gambler weaved sideways, slipped in a pool of Nigger Mike's blood and reeled off balance just as his opponent lashed out with a vicious right.

The blow landed with the slapping sound of a butcher's cleaver on a side of beef, catching the tall man high up on the cheek bone. He hurtled backwards, slamming against the table which went over in splintered ruin, and crashed to the floor. A wild yell burst from the Bar M punchers as he sagged over on his face and lay for a quivering instant.

But only for an instant. As the newcomer rushed forward, his face blazing with the mad light of battle, he lurched to his feet, bloody and disheveled, reeling a little, shaking his black head to free it of the mists that swirled across his brain. All the sunniness had left his gray eyes and they were cold as low clouds scurrying across a winter sky. He stopped the other's rush with a hard right to the mouth, sent him staggering back with a snapping left hook and jarred his head with another right. For a moment the two big men stood toe to toe and slugged. Then another terrific uppercut sent the newcomer reeling back.

With a startling suddenness the end came. The newcomer, both eyes swelling, his lips cut and bleeding, threw all caution to the wind and rushed madly. His opponent, himself bruised and bleeding, but icily cool, stooped and seized him about the thighs, hurling him over his shoulder with all the strength of his long arms added to the impetus of the other's wild rush.

It was as if the man had taken unto himself wings. The two battlers had changed position in the course of the fight and the newcomer had been facing the swinging doors. Clear through them he crashed, arms and legs revolving wildly. His head hit a passing fat Mexican in the belly, which fortunate occurrence doubtless saved him a broken neck but did not please the Mexican. The Mexican went end over end to the middle of the road, howling murder in two languages, and the human missile thudded on the sidewalk to lie motionless, arms widespread.

Almost instantly the tall gambler was beside the fallen man, concern darkening his bloody face. With swift, capable hands he felt him over for broken bones, prodding the dark curly head with slim, sensitive fingers, heaving a sigh of relief at not finding any evidence of a fracture. The fallen man breathed stertorously and still lay motionless. His opponent flung a single terse word over his shoulder—

"Water!"

Hogface Holliday brought it, and a towel. The tall man bathed the other's face, loosened the collar of his shirt and the handkerchief carelessly tied about his sinewy throat. More water and he groaned slightly, rolling his head from side to side.

Chet Madison, leaning forward with anxious eyes, offered advice—

"Slap his face, feller, that works sometimes in cases like this."

The other nodded and cuffed the unconscious man sharply on his lean cheeks. A louder groan rewarded his efforts, and more head rolling.

"That's the stuff!" exulted Madison. "Give him a coupla good ones!"

The tall man's slim hand cracked against the other's cheek, and again. Then he rocked back on his heels, his own ears ringing from the stinging slap of a firm little hand.

"You beast!" panted a furious voice. "You utter beast! Hitting a man when he's down and knocked out!"

The tall man raised his eyes to stare in amazement. Before him stood a girl, her blue eyes storming, her red hair seeming fairly to crackle with anger. She was small, with a graceful, rounded figure, a piquant face tanned sun-golden, a sweetly turned red mouth, and a tip-tilted little nose upon which a few freckles were visible.

"Good gosh!" the tall man heard Chet Madison breathe over his shoulder.

At that moment the unconscious man opened his eyes and sat up. He shook his head dazedly and stared at the girl. Her gaze flickered to his bruised face for an instant and returned to the tall man.

"Now leave him alone!" she blazed. "He's in no shape to fight back."

Her gaze, unutterably scornful, swept Chet Madison and the Bar M cowboys, who were grouped behind the tall gambler.

"I suppose you all jumped on him at once!" she exclaimed. "Well, it's just what would be expected of you!"

With that she was gone, turning abruptly on a small booted foot, her red head held high.

The man on the sidewalk stared after her and dazedly repeated Chet Madison's remark—

"Good gosh!"

His tall opponent, a grin twitching the corners of his rather wide, good-humored mouth, stood up and reached down a helping hand. The other got to his feet, somewhat unsteadily, still staring in the direction the red-haired girl had taken. His gaze turned to the man who had whipped him. He nodded in not unfriendly fashion.

"Well, that's that," he said, "looks sorta like yuh won the arg'ment, feller."

The other shook his head. "No," he replied soberly, "I think you won it. Your contention was that the Bar M is a man's outfit. Well, as you belong to it, and discounting that perforated misfit in there on the floor, it looks as though you've proved your point."

He turned to face Hogface Holliday, who was holding out his gunbelt.

"C'mon in and git washed up," invited the saloon-keeper, "yuh need it. The doc is workin' on Nigger Mike and says he'll be out and lookin' for a chanct to git hanged in a month."

The other man refused a similar invitation and he and the Bar M outfit started moving down the street toward a cowman's hotel. The tall gambler heard him voice a question before they were out of earshot—

"Who in blazes was that girl?"

And Chet Madison's reply, in an exceedingly dry voice—

"Name's Karen Walters. Her Ma was Teresa Gomez 'fore she married Bert Walters, who got killed the year after Teresa died. Teresa was one of the purtiest gals what ever come outa Mexico and Karen sorta takes after her. She lives with her grandpappy, Don Sebastian Gomez."

Chet's questioner shook his head in dismayed fashion and tossed his bloody handkerchief into the gutter.

"Who is that man?" the tall man asked Hogface Holliday.

Hogface shook his head. A cowboy leaning against the bar answered the question.

"I know him," said the cowboy. "He jest rode down from the Wyomin' country, where he's been livin' with his pappy who died not long back. Callate he ain't been in this section since he was a little shaver. That's old Anse McCoy's grandson, Sid McCoy."

Hogface's lips pursed in a soundless whistle. "Hell on top o' hell!" he grunted. He turned to the tall man as they walked to the back room, where water and towels were to be had.

"Seein' as names is bein' passed 'round sorta lib'ral like, what's yore handle, feller, if I ain't bein' too puh-sonal? Mine's Holliday, more common known as Hog-face."

The other glanced down at Holliday from his great height and his lips quirked humorously.

"Hatfield's my name," he replied. "Happens to be my real one, too. My friends generally call me Jim."

Chapter VIII

In the back room, Hogface Holliday, still chuckling reminiscently over the fight, bathed Jim Hatfield's bruised face.

"That one on the left cheekbone is the wuss—the one he landed when yuh was off-balance," Hogface said. "Yore mouth's cut a mite, but not 'nough to pay any 'tention to. A smidgeon of this hoss linament and yuh'll be all okay. Now let's eat—I wanta have a word with yuh, and I allus talk better on a full stomach."

"Clear this table off!" he bellowed to a swamper, "and then bring in some steaks and all the trimmin's!"

The steaks were soon forthcoming and a busy silence of some extent ensued. Hogface drained a final cup of scalding black coffee and heaved a long and satisfied sigh.

"I feel a sight better," he remarked. "Say, that was a slick little scheme Nigger Mike had cooked up, wasn't it?"

"Uh huh," Hatfield nodded, rolling a cigarette with the slim fingers of one hand. "Once the betting started and everybody got interested, he intended to change his hole card for that ace. Then when the showdown came and I showed two aces, the bottom one being the ace of spades, he'd turn over his own ace of spades and say I was cold decking the game. It would have looked bad for me as I'm a stranger hereabouts."

"Yeah, and wearin' a perfessional gambler's outfit," nodded Hogface. "Yuh ain't allus made yore livin' gamblin', though?"

It was really a statement, not a question, but Hatfield answered it.

"No, not always. I've done a few other things."

"Uh-huh, callate a rope ain't onfamiliar in yore hand," commented Hogface. "Well, cow chambermaidin' ain't over well paid, that's certain, and it's almighty hard work. That's how I happen to be in the liquor sellin' bus'ness. Ain't no sense in a man workin' hisself to death for nothin'. Me, I likes to eat reg'lar and often, and that costs money. And that brings me 'round to what I wanted to say in the fust place. I got a job for yuh, Hatfield, if yuh'll take it."

"What kind of job?"

"Dealer—dealer at that big-stake table. 'Bout three nights a week, fellers like the ones yuh was playin' with t'day, and fellers like Anse McCoy and even Don Sebastian Gomez—fellers with lots of money what ain't scairt to risk it—drap in for a game. Sometimes jiggers from the mines t'other side the river and over west of the Tinaja Hills set in the game, too. Yuh can't very well keep 'em out, but yuh can't allus be plumb sartain 'bout 'em. Now I don't want any more things happenin' like what happened t'day. That's a big game and the cut 'mounts to plenty, and I don't want to lose it. I got a rep'tation of runnin' straight games, and I wants to keep it. Yuh won't have much to do and yuh'll have lots of time to yoreself. Callate yuh'll be wantin' to look over the games in other places, and sich. I'll pay yuh top dealer wages to run that big game for me when it's in action. What yuh say?"

Hatfield considered swiftly. The proposition had its attractive features. His choosing the role of a gambler had not been by chance or idle inspiration. Long experience as a peace officer had taught him that the lawless, almost without exception, are addicted to gambling. Sooner or later, he felt sure, members of the sinister band that was causing the trouble in the Tinaja Basin would turn up at the gaming tables of Vegas, and cards and whisky are great looseners of tongues. As an habitué of the gaming tables, he would have an excellent chance of picking up valuable information. Hogface's offer simplified matters.

"All right," he told the saloonkeeper, "I'll take the job."

"Fine!" exulted Hogface. "I don't callate they'll be 'nother big game tonight, after what happened t'day, but come Friday the boys had oughta be pinin' for a little action. That'll give yuh two days to sorta rest up after the busy aft'noon yuh've had."

"Think I'll take a little ride tomorrow. What's the best way to get to the Cross P ranchhouse?"

"The Cross P, Nelson Page's outfit? Best way is to head almost due east from here till yuh pass Anse Mc-Coy's Bar M and then slant south a couple miles. That'll put yuh south of Don Sebastian's wire and a mile nawth of the river. Don Sebastian owns to the river, but when he fenced his range, he left that stretch to the south as a corridor for the spreads west of him. Decent feller, Gomez, no matter what some jiggers say 'bout him. After yuh pass the Regal range, foller the nawth fork of the trail and yuh can't miss the Cross P ranchhouse. Big white casa set on a hill in a grove of burr oaks. Was the old Turner place 'fore Page built it over, 'cordin' to his own ideas."

"What sort of fellow is Page?"

"Nice feller, jedgin' from all 'counts. Saw him onct. He drove over to town just as it was gettin' dark one night with a Chinaman feller what's his doctor. He didn't get outa the buckboard. Held the reins while the Chinaman feller went in and talked with Dent Crane, the sheriff. Heerd they was askin' Crane to try and stop the hell raisin' what's goin' on hereabouts. Somebody'd killed a couple their Mexican hands, or kidnapped 'em or somethin'. Anyway, they sorta disappeared and didn't show up again."

Hatfield nodded, his eyes somber. Holliday speculated his bruised face.

"Callate yuh'd better drop in at Doc Austin's office and have him take a stitch in that cut on yore cheek," the saloonkeeper advised. "It looks wus'n I figgered at fust and is liable to leave a bad scar. Might get dirt in it, too, gappin' open that way. Ain't no sense in takin' chances."

Hatfield agreed that the suggestion was good and had just got to his feet when the door opened and a frosty-eyed old man entered the room. He had a grizzled moustache, a blocky pair of shoulders and he wore a tarnished silver star on his sagging vest. Hogface nodded a greeting.

"Dent Crane, sheriff of the county," he offered. "Dent, this is Jim Hatfield. I jest hired him to deal my big poker table."

Crane nodded, giving Hatfield a keen glance.

"Wanted to get the straight of what happened here this af'noon," he said.

Hogface told him, with many profane comments. Crane listened without remark until the tale was finished.

"Looks sorta like Nigger Mike met his match for onct," he said with an approving nod. "Yuh made a almighty dangerous enemy, though, Hatfield," he added, "and the hull Bar M outfit is liable to back him up if it comes to a showdown."

Hogface chuckled with a sound like straight whisky gurgling from a bunghole.

"He walloped old Anse's grandson what's jest come down from Wyomin', and got his face slapped by Karen Walters, Don Sebastian's daughter's gal, too!"

"Good gosh!" exclaimed the sheriff. "Got the Bar M and the Regal outfits both lined up 'gainst yuh! Hatfield, my 'vice to you is to fork yore bronk and ride outa this deestrict while yuh're still in one piece. Yessuh, that's my advice!"

The Lone Wolf grinned, his gray eyes sunny. "Thanks," he said, "I'm not taking it."

"Callated yuh wouldn't," grunted Crane. "Well, drap in and see me when yuh take a notion. If I ain't in the office, Highpockets Hilton'll tell yuh when I'll get back, if yuh can ketch him awake."

Sheriff Crane departed and a little later Hatfield headed for the doctor's office.

"It'll be time to eat again when yuh get back," said Hogface. "I'll tell the cook to git busy."

The white-haired old doctor deftly closed the wound with a stitch or two.

"Nothin' to worry 'bout," he told the Ranger, "be healed in a coupla days. Thank yore lucky stars yuh ain't got somethin' like that pore devil laid out in there."

He jerked his thumb toward a sheeted form that lay on a table just beyond an inner door.

"Wanta see somethin' awful?" he asked.

A moment later, with crawling flesh, Jim Hatfield stared down at a replica of the mangled dying face he had gazed upon the night of the battle in the little river town.

"What caused it?" he asked, peering at the mutilated features, darkly Indian in coloring.

"Don't know," old Doc Austin replied. "If it wasn't for one thing, I'd say it was some sorta burn; but no burn would rot the jawbone and turn it inter a soft jellylike mass like that is. 'Pears like all the mineral matter of the bone is disintegrated or sorta melted down. I never in my life seed nothin' like it, and I ain't what yuh'd call 'zactly ign'rant 'bout diseases and poisons and sich."

Hatfield, glancing at the long rows of well-thumbed medical books that lined the walls of the inner room, was not inclined to dispute the point.

"Have you seen any more like this fellow?" he asked.

"No," Doc replied instantly, "and I don't wanta."

"Where'd he come from?"

"Couple Mexican fellers brought him in this mornin'. Jigger was dyin' and while I was workin' on him, the Mexicans snuk out. Highpockets Hilton, the dep'ty sheriff, was here helpin' me and he couldn't find hair or hide of 'em when he went lookin' for 'em. Nope, I never saw either one of 'em before; Highpockets didn't either."

Hatfield left Doc Austin's office in a serious mood. This latest specimen of the handiwork of the unknown raiders was disquieting in the extreme. It appeared to prove that they had in nowise been discouraged by their encounter with the Ranger, which had cost the lives of six of their number. They were undoubtedly still operating vigorously, and fatally.

The Lone Wolf was somberly thoughtful as he walked the roaring streets of the Border town. From time to time his glance shifted to the north, where those glowering hills fanged into the gold and scarlet evening sky. Deep purple shadows clothed their rugged slopes, softening the harsh lines, intensifying the air of sinister mystery that brooded over the raw drywash gashes and the black canyon mouths. Over the tallest crags seemed to writhe and hover a tremendous mist that from time to time refracted the bloody sunlight like a shifting cloud of diamond dust. A tenebrous filming of cloud it might be, Hatfield decided, although the sky above was clear as crystal and cleanly washed by the changing waves of color. It was as if the dark Spirit of the hills was glooming there above the lurid battlements of its grim castle of evil.

Between the town and the gloomy hills rolled the smiling rangeland, bathed in rose and amethyst and amber-tipped green, like a cheerful page of good deeds between two records of evil.

The First Chance was growing more uproarious by the minute. The long bar was crowded four deep. A corps of sweating bartenders sloshed raw whisky into glasses, often opening bottles by deftly knocking off the neck, which was speedier than pulling corks.

"Nothin' extra for busted glass, gents," they'd remark if a tinkle sounded in the course of the pouring. "Good for yuh, too—puts hair on yore chest!"

The customers seemed to think so, no complaints being registered against gritty fragments.

"Glass is easy on your innards, compared to what this likker does," bawled a big cowboy, sucking his long moustaches to get the last drop; "fill 'er up again and keep the bottle handy. Say! them gals on the dance floor is gettin' purtier ev'ry time I look at 'em through the bottom of this whisky glass!"

The dance floor was also crowded, there being hardly room for the couples to move. Bearded miners and lean-jawed cowboys tried to look soulful as they gazed into their partners' eyes, and the girls tried to look as if they believed it. The orchestra was bellowing forth "Buffalo Gals," and the click of high heels and the solid thump of boots kept lively time to the music.

The roulette wheels were also clicking merrily, and from the poker tables came the soft slither of cards as dealers expertly shuffled the decks. The big table in the corner, however, was vacant and a sheet covered its green cloth.

Hatfield found Hogface standing at the far end of the bar, gazing on the scene with pardonable pride.

"Purty, ain't it?" he beamed. "I callate they oughta be five, six nice fights 'fore come midnight. I got two new bungstarters this aft'noon, and 'nother box of shotgun shells. C'mon, yuh're jest in time to eat."

He led the way to the back room, where the table was already set. Hatfield hung his hat on a peg, smoothed his thick black hair with slim bronzed fingers and moved toward the table, which was placed near a window so as to profit as much as possible from the cool air flowing down from the hills. He had almost reached it when his keen eyes caught the momentary gleam of metal just outside the open window. A split second later his long body thudded face downward on the floor as the roar of a shot rocked the little room.

Chapter IX

Only a hairtrigger brain and muscles that instantly obeyed its impulses saved the Lone Wolf from death. He was hurtling sideways and down even as the charge of buckshot yelled through the air where his head had been the instant before. As he surged erect, to his quick ears came the thud of running feet outside the window.

Hatfield went through the window in a streaking dive. He landed on his feet, stumbled, recovered, and hurled himself toward a shadow a few yards distant. The fugitive was fast on his feet but the Ranger overtook him as if he were standing still. He whirled to meet his pursuer and the second barrel of the shotgun roared.

Hatfield felt the hot breath of the charge and the red blaze dazzled his eyes. He had a fleeting vision of two burning eyes set in a slabbing mask with only a blurred outline of human features. Then the darkness roared down and he closed with the other. The shotgun clattered to the ground and arms like bands of flexible steel wrapped the Ranger's body.

Never in his life had Jim Hatfield encountered such super-human strength. The man, almost as tall as the Ranger himself, was wide of shoulder and his body seemed made of iron wire. A surge of those mighty arms and the Ranger was lifted clear off his feet; but at the same moment his sinewy fingers closed on the other's throat, forcing his head back, throwing him off balance. The Ranger's great muscles swelled and writhed and the other's grip was burst asunder. Instantly one hand coiled about the Lone Wolf's wrist and he felt the skin rasp loose under the terrific torsion. One hand was torn free from the corded throat, a fist glanced against the

Ranger's jaw and the antagonists staggered apart.

From the darkness leaped another shadow. Hatfield ducked just in time to break the full force of a wicked blow launched at his head. Light blazed before his eyes and he reeled back, blinded.

There was a scurrying of swift feet in the darkness; the Ranger, shaking his head to clear his eyes, streaked both hands to his guns; but the two shadows whisked around the corner of a building and were lost amid a jumble of cabins and adobes that sprawled behind the larger structures fronting on the main street.

The whole thing had taken a scant ten seconds. Old Hogface Holliday had stormed through the window with as much speed as his bulk allowed. He came bellowing toward Hatfield, gun in hand. Hatfield told him briefly what had happened and Hogface swore a swirling blue streak with jagged crimson edges. He cocked an attentive ear to the Ranger's description of the apparently faceless man.

"I know a feller what might sorta answer that description," he rumbled. "He's got a face, all right, but it's all chopped up and might look like that in the dark. No, I ain't namin' no names, 'cause I ain't shore 'bout it and takin' a shot outa the dark at a man is mighty serious bus'ness, and I can't for the life of me figger why he'd be takin' a shot at yuh. Yuh'll see the jigger I'm thinkin' 'bout sooner or later, and I want yuh to be open-minded 'bout him. If he is the one, I callate yuh'll place him. C'mon back to the table. I callate they won't be no more damfoolishness t'night and it's long past time to eat."

Splintered ceiling boards showed where the buckshot charge had taken effect, but no other damage was apparent. The door of the inner room had been shut and the incident had not been noted amid the uproar in the saloon, the sound of a shot outside the building being too common an occurrence to attract attention.

Hatfield slept in a little room over the saloon that night, oblivious to the tumult downstairs. Whooping and shots in the street did not bother him either. But the vicious attempt on his life kept him awake and thoughtful for some time. Not for an instant did he doubt the reason for the attempt.

"They know me," he mused. "This gambler's get-up may fool others, but that faceless man got a good look at me that night in the river village and he isn't making any mistakes. Chances are, after failing to get me with that snake, they kept a watch on the place and had me trailed here. What they don't know is how much I know. They have no way of telling how much I found out that night in the village and they're taking no chances. They'll wipe me out if they get a chance. Well, I know where I stand now and that makes it easier for me and harder for them. Sooner or later they'll get nervous and tip off their hand. All I have to do is keep alive till that happens. Yes, that's all!"

The most disquieting circumstance was that while it was pretty apparent that the faceless man knew him for a Ranger, Hatfield as yet did not know who the faceless man was. So far he had but one clue, and that a vague one—the eyes in a dead man's face as he had seen them that night in the river village before the darkness of unconsciousness shrouded in his own eyes.

"I wish they hadn't done away with those bodies before I got well enough to take a look at them," he mused as his weary lids closed.

His horse was stabled nearby, and after breakfast the following morning he repaired to the livery stable and sought out the owner, a crippled ex-cowboy, Bandy Burton.

"Old Goldy's got a sore foot," he told Bandy, stroking the sorrel's glossy neck. "It isn't bad, but a rest of a few days won't hurt him. Have you anything I can hire for the day?"

Bandy nodded cheerfully. "Yuh can have that little bay in the far stall," he said. "A feller left him here last month in place of a feed bill he couldn't pay. Yuh can hire him, or yuh can have him for the price of the bill— it ain't much."

"I'll give him a trial today," Hatfield agreed. "Maybe I'll take him off your hands."

"I'd 'vise yuh use this heah saddle in place of yores," Bandy added. "It's a sight lighter and better fitted for this size of hoss. That sorrel just 'bout matches you for size. Golly, what a hoss!"

A little later the Ranger rode out of town, heading due east. The rented equipment proved satisfactory, especially as he did not anticipate any hard or fast riding.

"Just the same, I'll be glad when old Goldy is back in shape," he told himself. "Riding that horse is like having a full sized cyclone all ready to go into action, and cyclones aren't bad to have handy in case of emergencies."

A chance remark by Hogface Holliday had caused the Ranger to lay aside his long Colts with their heavy double cartridge belts.

"Them hawglegs shore show a lot of action," the old saloonkeeper had said, eying the smooth butts of the big guns with a speculative glance. "Can't say as I ever saw a gamblin' feller carry guns like that afore. Them's cowboy guns or I miss my guess."

Hatfield nodded without comment, but before he set out on his ride he changed the belt guns for a Smith & Wesson .45 taken from his saddlebags. The Smith was somewhat shorter in barrel and snugged smoothly into a shoulder holster concealed by the long black coat. The Lone Wolf was particular that any costume he might assume should present a harmonious whole.

"Little things like the wrong kind of guns are liable to give the whole show away to someone with sharp eyes," he reasoned.

So, apparently unarmed, he rode south of the rusty strands of wire which fenced Don Sebastian Gomez's great Regal ranch. As he rode, he speculated the stretch of rolling rangeland extending toward the misty outlines of the grim Tinaja Hills, and recalled in his mind's eye Hogface Holliday's instructions relative to the route he was to follow.

"Cutting across that fenced spread from the northeast would about halve the distance," he mused. "Well, we'll consider that when we head back this way."

A tall gate of ornamental iron broke the monotony of the onward marching wire. Hatfield could see a large white ranchhouse set amid a grove of ancient beeches—Don Sebastian Gomez's casa. With an appreciative eye the Ranger noted the tight barns, well-kept buildings and corrals.

"A real cowman," he decided. "Wonder if that's he riding toward the trail?"

Three mounted figures were trotting down the smooth road that wound from the gate to the ranch buildings, one slightly in front of the other two. A waiting wrangler opened the gate and the three riders sped briskly along the trail to meet the Ranger.

The leader was a tall man with dark piercing eyes, thick black hair liberally sprinkled with gray, a sensitive, high-nosed face notable for a firm, thin-lipped mouth and a stubborn jaw. Pride sat on that face, a high, even if intolerant, pride, and shone in every line of his slim, erect figure. He sat his coal black horse with the careless grace of one who has spent a lifetime in the saddle. His piercing glance took in the Ranger from head to foot as he drew near, but he said nothing and the expression on his face did not change. He drummed past Hatfield without nod or gesture of greeting.

Behind him rode a slim girl with hair like a forest pool brimful of sunset, and beside the girl rode a tall, sinewy man, dark of coloring, with lank black hair and blazing black eyes. His face was seamed and scarred with wounds, parts of the features appearing to have been whittled away. The Ranger recognized the work of small knives—such knives as are wielded deftly by the dusky hand of Apache or Yaqui when a prisoner is bound to the torture stake. Rarely indeed does a man walk or ride again after those knives have been at work on him, and the Ranger wondered what was the story of the man's experience. His dark brows drew together slightly and his eyes were coldly gray as he gazed on the scarred face. Instantly he knew that this was the man old Hogface Holliday had referred to in his veiled statement of the night before. Hatfield guessed the man to be an employee of Don Sebastian Gomez.

That the man in front was Don Sebastian himself, the Ranger did not doubt. He fitted perfectly all the descriptions he had heard of the *hidalgo*. The girl he recognized as Karen Walters, Don Sebastian's granddaughter.

The recognition was mutual. Hatfield saw the girl's red head go up and her blue eyes flash. Recalling the smack of that firm little hand against his bronzed cheek, Hatfield's lips quirked in an amused grin. The girl saw it as her horse swept abreast of him, and her face flushed angrily.

With courtly politeness, Hatfield doffed his wide hat. Karen shot him an indignant glance and rode on, her head still held high.

The sinewy Mexican riding beside the girl had not missed the bit of byplay and apparently attached more importance to the incident than the facts warranted. An expression of malignant hatred passed across his distorted features and he half turned in his saddle. Hatfield rode on without looking back.

A score of paces further on, the girl turned and for a fleeting moment gazed at the tall, erect figure lithely poised atop the bay horse. She faced front again with a peculiar expression in her wide eyes.

"Pedro," she said, her voice throatily sweet as the note of a mavis, "Pedro, I feel I ought to hate that man, but just the same, I'd rather be *slapped* by him than kissed by any other man I ever knew!"

Pedro Zorrila swore an amazed Spanish oath back of his yellow teeth.

"Me, I would rather be slapped by the mountain lion or the great bear than by heem!" he declared with conviction.

CHAPTER X

HATFIELD would have chuckled had he seen the second meeting enjoyed by Don Sebastian's party; it occurred on the outskirts of Vegas.

A half dozen cowboys, superbly mounted, swept into town, laughing and chatting among themselves. They came face to face with the party from the Regal ranch and silence like a wet wooly blanket fell upon them. It was broken by the tall, broad-shouldered young man who rode in front, a young man who was undoubtedly astonishingly handsome of feature, under normal conditions. Now, however, he was the possessor of two gorgeous black eyes, a swollen nose, puffed lips and a magnificent lump on the side of his lean jaw. Just the same, however, the eyes glowed and the lips spread in what was intended for a smile as he sighted Karen Walters. He swept his wide hat from his head, revealing hair whose beauty had not suffered from contact with the Lone Wolf's fists.

"Mawnin', Ma'am!" he greeted, his voice somewhat thick because of slightly loosened teeth.

Karen, her furious eyes on Chet Madison and those accompanying him, passed by as if she had not heard. Don Sebastian's back was stiff as a ramrod. Pedro Zorrila glared murder. Sid McCoy's jaw sagged.

"It ain't you in particular, Sid," said Chet Madison, with a bushy chuckle, "it's the comp'ny yore in—that is, if she ain't found out yet that the Old Man's yore grandpappy. Yuh can't 'spect a Gomez gal to look fav'ble on a Bar M man. Purty though, ain't she, for a greaser gal!"

Madison was about as tough as they make them, but

he shied back from the blaze of Sid McCoy's eyes.

"I ain't wantin' to hear yuh make any more 'greaser' cracks when speakin' of her!" he rasped between his teeth. "Unstan'?"

Chet met McCoy's crackling glare for an instant, then his snapping little eyes shifted aside.

"I didn't mean nothin'," he muttered. "What's eatin' yuh, anyhow?"

Sid McCoy said nothing more, but the lines in his bruised face did not immediately smooth out. Chet Madison glanced sideways at him, intense speculation in his gaze: Chet could see through a mill stone when there was a hole in the middle.

"Now if *this* don't beat the devil!" he mumbled in the wilderness of his whiskers.

The Turner ranchhouse had been old when Caleb Turner bought it from its Mexican owner, and that was fifty years before Nelson Page took over the Cross P from Caleb's heirs. It was a vast rambling structure of creamy adobe and white stucco, built around a spacious patio where a fountain sprayed amid blazing banks of flowers. A grove of burr oaks surrounded the house, their gnarled monotony relieved by an occasional beech or cottonwood. Nelson Page had added many modern improvements in the interest of comfort to the hacienda, and had enhanced its natural beauty with tasteful decorative features. The barns and other supplementary buildings were in excellent condition.

"Another man who knows how a spread should be kept," Hatfield decided as he walked the horse up the winding gravel roadway.

A sprucely attired Mexican appeared from nowhere and took his horse. Another waited at the head of the wide veranda and hastened to announce his presence. A moment's delay and he was led through a wide cool hall and ushered into a lofty room whose black velvet hangings enhanced its shadowiness. It was the kind of a room the old Dons designed to alleviate the heat of a near tropical summer and to protect from the cold of winter blizzards that all too frequently swept down from the northwest.

The great room was sparsely, almost austerely furnished, which increased the impression that it harmonized perfectly with the man who sat behind a huge dark desk, even as he had sat that day, more than two months before, when old Manuel Cardenas came to him pleading help for the man who now approached the desk, his keen eyes taking in the white expressionless face, the deepset dark eyes burning with intelligence, the broad shoulders. Beside Page, even as on that other day, stood Tsiang, the huge Chinese physician, to whom, according to the account of the old Mexican doctor, Jim Hatfield owed his life.

Tsiang nodded his magnificently shaped head in greeting. Nelson Page's head also inclined, very slightly. His face, inscrutable in the shadow, mirrored no emotion whatsoever. Neither spoke.

It was one of the Lone Wolf's rules never to open a conversation if it were possible not to do so. Here, however, he felt that the burden was upon him and that he could not very well do otherwise.

"Mr. Page?" he questioned, "Doctor Tsiang?"

Tsiang bowed with stately courtesy. The Cross P owner spoke in his sonorous, vibrant voice:

"I am Nelson Page."

The Ranger nodded, and continued: "I don't think either of you need to be told who I am. Probably Dr. Tsiang recognized me without any trouble, even if I have changed from when he saw me last. I'm here to thank you both for what you did for me—if it weren't for Dr. Tsiang, I wouldn't be here at all, and I understand, Mr. Page, that it was at your request that the doctor looked after me."

Tsiang inclined his head in acknowledgment. Page stared straight into the Ranger's eyes.

"You profited by a mistake, Mr. Hatfield—that is your name, I believe—a mistake on my part and a certain amount of deception on the part of your friend Cardenas. As an individual, I am utterly indifferent toward you, sir, but as a representative of the race that endeavored to defraud and murder me and left me a cripple, I would hardly have interceded with Dr. Tsiang in your behalf. I am telling you this, Mr. Hatfield, to make my attitude clear."

"You are a member of that race yourself, sir," the Ranger commented quietly.

Page nodded. "I am," he admitted, "by accident of birth. I may add what you have left unspoken, that I am a renegade, a traitor to my kind. That is doubtless the thought in your mind. The truth of the matter is, I am neither. I am merely disgusted and nauseated by the treachery and ingratitude I have met with at the hands of my own kind. Men who were beholden to me for great favors tried to ruin me, hiding behind the hackneyed excuse—'business is business.' A man I took into my home when he was friendless and in poverty engineered the plot which resulted in my near death. Dr. Tsiang, a yellow man, saved my life, even as he saved yours. I looked about me and saw that the submerged races, the 'lesser tribes without the law,' were the constant victims of white exploitation. Here in this Border country is an outstanding example of that which I speak. Relative to yourself, word came to me just today that you recently committed a vicious assault upon a representative of the humble people of this section and left him near death. Is it not so?"

He leaned forward slightly, placing both hands on top of the gleaming desk, the light from the shaded student lamp beating full upon them.

Hatfield's gaze instinctively followed the gesture. For a moment his glance remained fixed; then he raised his level gray eyes to meet Nelson Page's accusing stare.

"I don't think the man you are speaking of will die—yet," he replied.

Page, evidently expecting explanations and excuses, seemed somewhat taken aback. Tsiang nodded like an animated Buddha and there was a slight gleam in his obsidian eyes.

Nelson Page leaned back in his chair and there was a

flicker of what might be interpreted as approval in his own dark eyes. His voice changed subtly and he spoke as if all that had passed was dismissed from his mind.

"I regret the inconvenience of having to work at present," he said. "Doctor Tsiang will act as host in my place and will doubtless be pleased to have you share his luncheon."

Tsiang nodded and smiled.

Hatfield hesitated a moment, then nodded acceptance. After all, he could hardly refuse the invitation without appearing boorish.

"Thank you, sir," he said.

Page made no reply and Hatfield followed the Chinese doctor to a smaller room where a table was already set for two.

The meal, served by a soft-footed Chinese, was a good one and Hatfield enjoyed it. Tsiang conversed pleasantly, choosing topics of general interest to the rangeland country, speaking in his precise, somewhat stilted English. He was the perfect host.

Upon leaving the table, they did not pass through the lofty room in which Nelson Page sat behind his great desk, Tsiang leading the way into a corridor which turned into the shadowy hall.

Hatfield's horse was waiting for him at the veranda steps. He mounted, bade the Chinese goodbye and rode toward the trail. Tsiang watched him until his figure was small in the distance, then slowly reentered the house, his face thoughtful.

Another mile of riding and Hatfield pulled the bay horse to a halt. Before stretched the strands of rusty wire which encircled the Regal ranch. The trail turned sharply here, slanting to the south to where, miles distant, it would turn sharply west again.

The Ranger glanced at the sky. He and the Chinese doctor had lingered long over the meal and the day was already far advanced. It would be well after dark before he could hope to reach Vegas, following the roundabout way of the trail, and Hogface had mentioned the possibility of a game at the high stakes table that night.

On the other hand, a short cut across the Regal spread would just about halve the distance. Jim Hatfield, himself a product of the open range, did not look with particular favor on wire, especially when the fence was admitted to be, to some extent at least, a grudge fence. Shrugging his wide shoulders, he continued to ride due west, ignoring the southward slanting trail. Soon he pulled up the bay beside the fence. He chose a post the wood of which was somewhat rotted.

A few wrenches of his steely fingers and the staples holding the rusty barbed wire were loosened. He carefully led the bay across the sagging strands, replaced the staples, mounted and cantered westward across the rolling range of the Regal ranch.

And high on their mountain thrones, the evil gods of the Tinaja Hills chuckled sardonically as the Lone Wolf rode to his unexpected rendezvous with death.

Chapter XI

Sunset flamed above the Tinaja Hills and their ragged battlements seemed washed with a bloody froth. Further down, the cliffs were stained a deep wine whose purple dregs were the shadows that coiled about their feet. Emerald and amber glowed the rangeland, fading to misty blue as the graying powder of the dusk sifted down from the color-washed sky impalpably to tint waving grass blade and trembling flower. The hush of newborn stars brooded over the waiting earth and as the little shadows lost themselves in the darkening arms of twilight, the winds were silent and the very gossamers were still. Peace rested upon the rangeland, the sweet peace of tired nature seeking rest.

Peace, except in the hearts of men. Far to the south, where a bristle of stunted trees stood just inside the Regal wire, from which the long stretch of the trail could be seen plainly, a group of solider shadows clustered—mounted men, silent, motionless, save for the occasional soft thud of an impatiently pawing hoof or the faint jingle of bridle irons. East and west stretched the trail, dimming to furtive gray in the fading light, lonely, deserted.

The waiting group suddenly tensed. A dot had appeared on the gray shimmer, a dot that swiftly grew to a speeding horseman. The watchers leaned forward in their saddles; a rope in a sinewy hand coiled snakily. A voice suddenly gutturaled—

"That is not him!"

Low mutterings arose, then exclamations of recognition as the horseman slowed, called out, and halted his panting horse where the tree clump formed a pool of

74

shadow on the trail. He leaned across the fence, his voice shaking with excitement.

"He comes not this way," speaking Spanish with a strange lilting accent. "He lowered the wire where the trail turns south and rode across the range. From the shelter of a grove I watched and saw."

A chorus of curses in more than one language arose. The uproar was stilled by a peremptory voice—

"It matters not. Our task will be the simpler. Well it is that I place one to watch against the time he should ride back to town."

"You did well," the voice called to the mounted man in the trail.

A harshly barked word of command and the group got under way with a low thunder of swift hoofs. North by east they rode, toward where the last flames of sunlight flickered and died upon the bleak peaks of the Tinaja Hills.

The Lone Wolf rode warily across the Regal ranch. He was aware that Don Sebastian and his riders would resent his trespass upon the fenced range. He knew, however, that the ranchhouse and other buildings lay far to the south of the route he was pursuing. With the time of year and the lateness of the hour considered, his chances of meeting with any of the Regal hands was negligible. If he did encounter some of the Lazy R riders, he could plead his status of a stranger in the locality, an excuse which would doubtless be accepted, albeit perhaps with poor grace.

In addition to his desire for a short cut to town, Hatfield was curious about the fenced range. He wondered if there might not be some reason other than the purported desire for isolation which prompted Don Sebastian to go to such trouble and expense. The Lone Wolf was beginning to build a theory of explanation relative to the sinister happenings in the Tinaja Basin, a theory built upon a fragile foundation of small incidents, things that would have passed unheeded by a man of less keen perceptions. On the face, his deductions

seemed preposterous, and he lacked a concrete govern-
ing motive; but long experience had taught the Lone
Wolf that sane and logical motives were not always
vitally essential where the lawless were concerned.

"When men get to hating other men, their thinking
processes slip off the straight trail and get bogged down
in all kinds of funny ways," he mused. "You never can
tell what a man who hates someone else or feels he's
been wronged will do, or how he'll do it. When men
feel that way or want things they have no right to,
there's nothing you can tie to when you start figuring
why they do what they do. You have to take your
chances and trust to luck."

The last of the sun fires had flickered out and only a
tremulous saffron glow hovered over the tallest clouds,
that and the intangible wavering mist the Ranger had
noticed the evening before. His dark brows drew together as he gazed at it ere the wan glow died and vanished. There was something sinister and threatening
about that nebulous curdling of the dregs of dead light.
Again the feeling came to Hatfield that this was the
wandering ghost of the evil Spirit of the hills, abroad
once more upon some fell mission of its own, a malign
influence, motivating the human actors on this green
stage of the rangeland. His lips quirked humorously at
the thought and with a shrug of his wide shoulders he
brushed it aside; but he could not altogether throw off
the feeling of depression and disquietude it engendered.
The man who rides with danger ever his saddle companion develops, to an uncanny degree, that inexplicable sixth sense that warns of impending events. With
that unseen monitor clamoring in his brain, Hatfield
rode, wary and alert, eyes and ears missing nothing.

A moon like a gigantic orange was slowly climbing
the long slant of the eastern sky, flooding the prairie
with amber light, blocking the shadows in solid ebony.
The palely golden glow flowed furtively about a clump
of chaparral that clung to the side of a swelling rise and
slightly to the left of the Ranger's path. Beneath the
low branches of the stunted trees the gloom was intense.

It was only the faintly musical jingle of a bridle iron, but to the Ranger, every sense keenly alert, it was enough. He was slewing sideways in his saddle as a rope swished snakily from the gloom beneath the trees.

The throw was a good one and but for that tinkle of metal the instant before, the tight loop would have settled about the Lone Wolf's shoulders. As it was, the twine brushed his arm and smacked the bay horse smartly on the flank. He leaped high with a snort of indignation. Hatfield, recovering instantly, drove his spurs home.

"Hate to do it, fellow," he apologized to the bay.

His hand streaked to the big gun under his left armpit and the reports rolled like drum beats as he raked the thicket with lead. That deadly swish of coiled rope was challenge enough for the Lone Wolf.

Yells and shouts answered the crash of the Smith, and a long shriek of agony. The whole front of the thicket flickered flame and slugs howled about the speeding rider. Then the thudding drum of fast hoofs in pursuit. Hatfield, leaning low in the saddle, his attention riveted on the broken ground ahead, cursed the mischance that deprived him of his big sorrel in this moment of dire need.

"With old Goldy it would be a joke," he muttered, "but this horse isn't built for speed and there's nothing funny about it!"

The unexpected blaze of gunfire in their very faces had momentarily thrown the drygulchers into confusion and had given the Ranger a start. Now, however, better mounted, they were closing the distance. To Hatfield's surprise, after that initial instinctive reply to his volley, the pursuers held their fire. He pondered this as he reloaded. The effect was disquieting.

"Looks as though they know they got me where they want me," he grunted, his quick gaze roving back and forth across the moonlit range.

Ahead, shadowy in the paling light, was a straggling line of trees and brush, broken in spots, stretching uniformly from north to south. Hatfield's eyes narrowed at the sight. It might mean a stream, but there was no glint of water to indicate the presence of one. High steep banks, perhaps, difficult to ride down. That might explain the seeming confidence of the pursuit.

"Looks like you'll have to try your hand at a little diving," he told the bay. "We won't be held up by any mud puddles."

In the nick of time he realized what was before him. Almost beneath the horse's nose yawned the black gash of Devil Canyon.

Hatfield jerked the bay about in a hairpin turn. He must ride along the rim of the canyon, seeking shelter amid the straggle of growth.

"No wonder they are taking it easy," he muttered. "They knew all along they had me cornered."

The bay came about gallantly in answer to the bridle; but at the moment all four feet were planted on a glaze of glassy rimrock. His legs went from under him as if he were roped and he crashed to the ground on his side.

By a miracle of agility, Hatfield got his leg from beneath the falling horse, but he was completely off balance and he was hurled from the saddle and yards distant.

Through a blaze of whirling lights and roaring sound, he dimly heard clattering hoofs and triumphant yells. A moment later all the light went out under a wave of chill darkness.

Chapter XII

His mind groping in the cold borderland between consciousness and insensibility, Hatfield vaguely realized a confused panorama of kaleidoscopic happenings. There was a jerking, swaying descent, with feet thudding dully on damp stone steps, a long jolt through rocky corridors ringing with echoes, and the moan and mutter of swift-rushing water, with the cool night air pleasant on his face after the dank breath of subterranean passages. A blank followed, when the cold blackness swathed his brain, fold on fold. Then more corridors of stone, a period of blinding, sweltering heat that rocked and trembled to a vast and deep-toned roaring; flashes of dazzling light and finally rest under a peaceful glow, with the ear-numbing roar deadened and muffled to a mighty rushing murmur that vibrated the air but was so close to the nadir of utter silence as to be soothing like deepest organ notes.

The return to full consciousness was gradual and not particularly pleasant. His head ached abominably and he felt stiff and sore all over. The fall from the horse had been a hard one and there was a limit to what even the iron physique of the Lone Wolf could endure.

"Feel as though I'd been pulled through a splintery knothole and hung on a barbed wire fence to dry," he told himself as he stretched his cramped limbs, dimly realizing that the surface beneath him was yielding and not unpleasant. Flexing his arms, he was thankful to be assured that no bones were broken.

"Must have landed on my head," he decided. "Otherwise, the chances are I'd have cashed in my chips. I was in the air so long I thought I'd grown wings!"

Opening his eyes was a painful process at first and he quickly closed them after the first attempt. Then, the pinwheels and skyrockets having subsided somewhat, he tried it again, and stared straight at a rocky ceiling bathed in a reddish glow.

It was a lofty ceiling with a vaulted appearance, and a single glance sufficed to tell the Ranger that it was living rock and not cut or placed by hands—the ceiling of a cavern. Staring at it, Hatfield recalled the vague impressions that had thronged his numbed mind before the last period of black unconsciousness, impressions of echoing rocky corridors and dank stone steps.

"Still underground!" he muttered. "Now what the—"

His conjecture abruptly died unfinished and his intelligence, keenly alert once more, concentrated on a matter close at hand. He had not yet turned his head nor shifted his gaze from the rocky vault above, but he knew that eyes rested upon him. For a moment he lay undecided, then slowly he shifted his gaze to the right. Seated near the bunk on which he lay was a shadowy figure. Realizing that the watcher had undoubtedly noted his return to consciousness, he turned his head and met the glowing black stare that was fixed unwinkingly on his face.

The man who sat on the bench beside the bunk was tall and broad of shoulder, swathed in a dark Mexican serape. A gauzy handkerchief of dark silk was about his throat, a wide sombrero on his head.

Of his face, little but the glowing dark eyes could be seen, a fold of the handkerchief being looped about the lower portion; but through the filmy silk, the Ranger could make out a grotesque shapelessness, as if most of the face had been cut or burned away, leaving only blurred outlines and horrid distortion. Powerful, sinewy hands rested upon his knees and as Hatfield's glance took them in, he instinctively knew that these were the hands that had come so near to crushing the life from his body in the alley back of Hogface Holliday's saloon. Yes, sitting beside the bunk on which he lay was the dread *Hombre sin Cara*, the Man without a Face!

Quietly the Ranger lay, but with every muscle of his long body tense, waiting for the other to speak. He did so, in a deep voice with a peculiar bell-like quality; the words were precise, unaccented Spanish:

"Doubtless you are surprised that you are still alive?"

Hatfield knew it was a waste of time to pretend ignorance of Spanish so he replied in the same language—

"Really hadn't thought about it one way or the other."

The other nodded his muffled head. "No, doubtless you wouldn't. It is surprising, though, don't you think?"

Before replying, the Ranger sat up, not without a whirling of his head and a sickish feeling in the pit of his stomach. The nausea passed in a moment, however, and he swung his long legs over the edge of the bunk and rested his back against the rock wall against which it was built.

"No, it isn't, not now," he replied. "When I came to enough to realize I was being carried somewhere, I didn't worry about being killed in a hurry. You wouldn't go to all that trouble to kill me. If that'd been the idea, you'd have done away with me right after I tumbled out of my saddle."

The other nodded appreciation of the shrewd reasoning. "Texans of your type seldom lack intelligence," he remarked. "No, I did not have you brought here for the purpose of killing you, at least not immediately and without reason. I had you brought here because I have a proposition to offer you, one that should prove singularly attractive to any man in his right mind; the alternative we will discuss later. First, however, I wish to warn you against any meditated attack upon my person. I have been at grips with you, as you well know, and I do not underestimate your prowess. Glance beyond me and you will see how ill advised such an attempt would be."

Hatfield nodded. His quick eyes had already taken in the swarthy armed men who stood only a few paces distant, their faces in the shadow, their backs to the soft glow that poured through openings high in the rock wall of the cavern room, which the Ranger now saw to be of no great extent.

"Why did you change your mind?" he asked the faceless man. "You tried hard enough to kill me the other night. I can still hear the buckshot whistling over my head."

"My intention was to kill you," the other replied frankly, "for I considered you dangerous. A revised estimate of your ability decided me that you might prove equally valuable if handled right. I have need of men of your calibre."

Hatfield said nothing, but the expression in his level eyes changed slightly. The other went on, apparently not noticing.

"You may wonder what all this is leading to; I will tell you. I have discovered one of the great secrets of nature. Largely by chance I hit upon one of her storehouses of vast wealth. Circumstances and conditions into which I will not go at present, make the garnering of that wealth a matter of great difficulty and danger. Profound secrecy is of the utmost importance; but I need men of ability and courage to assist me. Such men are not easy to come by. For the lesser tasks, I have little difficulty in enlisting recruits."

"By way of the Mexican river towns, for instance," Hatfield remarked quietly.

The other nodded without emotion. "Yes, labor can be recruited there. Now and then chance throws an acceptable offering my way, men who can be, ah, induced to fall in with my plans."

"And these who came back to the river towns—did they get in the shape they were in by doing your work?" the Ranger questioned, his voice still quiet.

The other leaned forward and Hatfield could see a subtle change come over him. His eyes glowed more brightly, his voice took on a brittle edge.

"Those," he said, slowly and distinctly, "were ones who opposed me and who had to be taught a lesson—a lesson which would serve chiefly as an example to others. Do I make myself clear?"

Hatfield nodded. "And you had me brought here in order to enlist me in this scheme, whatever it is?"

"Yes," the other replied. "When you rode to visit the Señor Page you were watched and followed, and the trap into which you rode was laid for you. I thought for a moment we had lost you when you evaded the rope and my men instinctively answered your fire. I don't see how they missed."

"Just luck, I guess," said the Ranger. "Well, just what is this proposition you are offering me?"

"I am offering you," the other said slowly, "wealth beyond your wildest dreams, and power and place and the mastery over men and material things. I don't underestimate your latent ability and I know you can be of the greatest assistance to me. As I said before, you have what your type usually possesses—the ability to recognize opportunity and make the most of it, particularly so where it applies to your own lives. That ability means the ability to get things done. I am opportunity."

Hatfield's steady eyes had never left the other's face. Now he spoke, softly, quietly.

"You know," he said, "that reminds me of a jest made to a man once about two thousand years ago. He was offered 'the Power and the Glory' of the world, and mastery over all sorts of things by one who claimed to be opportunity. Do you remember the story?"

The other leaned closer, his dark eyes burning brightly, and the brittle bell notes were back in his voice when he spoke, still in Spanish.

"There is only one difference, according to the telling of that fable, in His experience and yours. He was taken onto a mountain. You, amigo, have been taken into one."

The Ranger's lips quirked appreciation of the other's quickness of understanding and the fineness of the distinction.

"Just the same," he replied quietly, "the answer you are getting is what that other fellow got who came bringing opportunity."

The faceless man leaned back. "I had hoped," he said,

"that you would profit by *His* mistake. Do you recall the final chapter of the story? The fate which awaits those who oppose me is worse than crucifixion."

Before Hatfield could answer, he rose to his feet. "Come," he said, "I have certain things to show you before accepting your refusal as final. Perhaps you can be prevailed upon to change your mind."

The Ranger stood up and was pleased to find himself steady on his feet once more. The other turned his back on him and led the way toward an opening in the rock wall. The armed retainers silently swung in behind the pair. Four of them, Hatfield counted, each with dark, sinewy hand on ready gun butt.

They entered the corridor, which was duskier than the room. The air vibrated to the swelling notes as of a mighty organ.

"What's that noise?" Hatfield asked the man beside him.

"We are very near to the earth's eternal fires," the other replied. "What you hear is the rushing flames in the heart of the mountain."

The corridor wound on for many yards. As the little party progressed, the rushing roar grew louder, the light increased, and at the same time the temperature rose sharply. The heat was sweltering when they rounded a final turn and a burst of intense light dazzled their eyes after the comparative gloom of the corridor.

For a moment Hatfield could make out nothing other than leaping flames and moving shadows; then his vision accustomed to the change and he glanced about with consuming interest.

They stood on the threshold of a vast room, a mighty natural cavern carved out from the heart of a mountain by the rushing flames and exploding gases. Close to the far wall, pillars of writhing fire shot from openings in the rocky floor, to lose themselves in other openings in the roof, far, far overhead. These, Hatfield quickly deduced, were flaming gases escaping from the inferno below. They filled the cavern with a hot white glow, in which moving men were outlined in the utmost detail.

Hatfield saw other jets of flames—smaller jets that blazed and flared under great iron crucibles somewhat similar to the crucibles of a steel mill. In the crucibles something bubbled and boiled, giving off unpleasant choking fumes. On stone platforms built beside the huge pots, men, stripped almost naked, sweat gleaming on their dark skin, stirred the mixture with huge iron ladles. Other men bore sacks of yellowish or glistening brown ore and dumped them into the containers. Along the walls stood watchful guards, rifles in their hands. Others of the dark-faced guards walked beside the staggering burden bearers. Hatfield eyed the armed watchers with narrowing eyes.

"Yaqui Indians, most of 'em," he muttered under his breath, "but not all—not all!"

The look in his gray eyes was exultant as he noted those other watchers who were not Indians. "It's beginning to tie up," he told himself. "It's beginning to tie up tight!"

He glanced about the glowing room. The walls were massive beds of sandstone. Near the base of the walls were to be observed long, narrow seams or lenses of greenish shale. Above these were, invariably, veins of ore of a mottled yellow and brown coloring, with occasional showings of glistening black. There were also strange-appearing outcroppings, cylindrical "trees" or "logs" of ore of a brilliant yellow.

Excitement was welling in the Ranger's mind. Also vague memory stirrings. There was something illusively familiar, and peculiarly significant, about these unusual ore formations. He conned over his geology and mineralogy with his mind's eye, but without immediate success. He could not for the moment catalogue the outcroppings. That the contents of the sacks borne by the staggering laborers were identical with the mysterious veins, he felt sure. He turned a mildly curious face to his companion.

"What do you have here—gold?" he asked.

The fold of silk across the unseen face moved slightly, as if the distorted lips were smiling.

"Yes, I have—gold!" was the reply.

Without further comment he led the way diagonally across the room, to the edge of a vast pit from which beat a sullen reddish glare. Hatfield glanced over the edge and down—down, depth upon vertiginous depth, to where blazed and coiled and hissed and sparkled what appeared to be a lake of intense fire. Writhing vapors, like souls in torment, drifted over the luridly glowing surface and across Hatfield's mind flashed a vision of that sinister shadow which hovers over the topmost crags of the Tinaja Hills. He believed now that he knew what caused that strange cloud-like shadow.

His companion turned from the seething cauldron in the pit.

"There," he said significantly, "is the end of many things." Hatfield nodded his understanding. The other led the way to an opening in the rock wall some distance from the pit. The armed guards kept steady step, drew a little closer. One struck a light to a torch which burned with a smoky, resinous flame, casting a fitful light upon the glistening stone floor, the darkly shining walls. Quite a distance was traversed before they came to a wooden door set in the living rock. This was pushed open and they entered a small rock-walled room in which an oil lamp burned with a steady glow.

Hatfield glanced about with interest. The room appeared to be a combination laboratory and study. Books lined the walls. On a long table were retorts, braziers, test tubes, racks of shining instruments.

Something else on that table caught the Ranger's eye and held it for a fleeting moment of intense concentration. On a tray lay ten small objects of gleaming silver. They were convexly oval in shape, formed like rings with an inner segment removed. Hatfield, whose years of varied experience had brought him into touch with many unusual things, instantly recognized them for what they were.

"Fingernail protectors!" flashed through his mind; "and there's only one kind of man I ever heard tell of wearing those things!" They were, he exultantly realized, another link in the chain he was forging from small, apparently inconsequential incidents and facts. Small things in themselves—the veins on the back of a hand, a dead man's face, a muttered curse, the staring glance of a watchful guard.

"Little things, uh-huh," the Lone Wolf's keen mind exulted, "but put them all together and they're strong enough to kick the gallows drop from under the feet of a murdering devil!"

The faceless man gestured to a blanket-covered couch. He seated himself in a roughly made chair, facing the Ranger.

"What you just saw will be explained when, and if, you join forces with me," he said. "Now we will discuss the alternative proposition."

He paused, his eyes burning blackly above the fold of silk. The armed men flanked him on either side, their swarthy faces expressionless, their eyes glittering. Hatfield waited, saying nothing. The other shot a question—

"You recall the dying man you saw in the river village, and the body of the man who died in the doctor's office at Vegas?"

Hatfield nodded, wondering what was coming next. The other leaned forward.

"Those men opposed their will to mine," he said slowly. "You saw what happened to them. That also happened to others. Death came slowly to them, and terribly. That is the alternative I am offering you!"

CHAPTER XIII

FOR a long moment Hatfield sat staring into the other's burning eyes—the eyes of a madman. There was no doubt in his mind but that the man was capable of carrying out his threat. The other waited, expectant, for the Ranger's answer.

It came in a way he did not in the least expect. The Lone Wolf left the couch like a coiled spring. His iron-hard fist lashed at the fold of silk and sent the faceless man, chair and all, crashing to the floor. He knocked one of the armed guards senseless and sent another hurtling against the long table. The others closed like hounds with a mountain lion.

With the convulsive strength that comes from the spirit rather than from the body, Hatfield bore the yelling, fighting quartette almost to the closed door of the room. It was the hand of the faceless man, snaking out from below, that jerked his feet from under him and brought him crashing to the floor. He was quickly smothered under the weight of hard bodies, his arms and legs pinioned by muscular hands. Breathing hard, he was hauled to his feet and held fast.

His captors were also breathing hard, and muttering curses. The faceless man, a stain of blood on the swathing of silk, rasped a harsh command.

Quickly the Ranger's coat was stripped from his shoulders. The left sleeve of his shirt was rolled up, revealing a sinewy arm with the great muscles lying smooth and flat under the glossy skin. The faceless man moved to the racks on the long table, chose a shining instrument and a stoppered vial. He stepped to the helpless Ranger, gripped the bared arm with fingers like rods of steel.

Hatfield felt a searing pain, like the rasp of a file or the slither of a hot iron, a moment of intense irritation on quivering raw flesh and then the faceless man stepped back. Still wordless, he procured cotton and gauze and deftly bandaged the wounded arm. A gesture, and the guards rolled down the sleeve and replaced the coat. The faceless man spoke.

"I have inoculated you with the disease from which those men died," he said, his voice flat and emotionless. "When you feel the virus stirring within your veins, think upon what I have said. And remember—I and I alone know the cure for the affliction. Think on that, also."

Calling one of the guards aside, he spoke to him in rapid Spanish. The guard grunted gutturally, turned and prodded the Ranger with the muzzle of his gun. The guards keeping firm hold on his arms, Hatfield was thrust from the room and hurried down the torch-lighted corridor.

Every sense alert, the Ranger noted the guards instinctively shy away from a second closed door some distance down the corridor. Another moment or two and they were at the mouth of the tunnel.

Apparently dawn was just breaking and the scene that met the Ranger's eyes was bathed in pale light. Near the mouth of the tunnel was a jumble of small rough buildings and sheds, under which could be seen bits of rusty machinery. One building, he noted, was rudely daubed with red warning signs "Dynamite," the signs spelled in Spanish. This building perched precariously on the near bank of a swiftly rushing stream, quite narrow, but apparently of great depth. A path stretched steeply up from the cave mouth to the bank of the stream. Hatfield judged the level of the water to be slightly higher than the floor of the corridor. The banks of the stream were solid rock of a basaltic nature.

Glancing up, Hatfield suddenly realized that the time was not early morning but near or after midday.

He could see, framed in jagged stone, a narrow strip of blue sky and a gleaming eye of sun.

He was, in fact, at the bottom of a narrow gorge of immense depth. Full two thousand feet reared glistening black cliffs, naked save where long stringers of gray moss, like the beard on a dead man's face, clung to the stone. A warm glow touched the far-off summits of the beetling crags, but here at their base was murky grayness. It was as if only the curdled heavier dregs of light found their way into the immense depths. No bright winged sunbeam could fall so far; they died far, far above and their wan ghosts struggled feebly against the rising shadows. Eerie echoes ran along the frowning bastions and faded to far away sibilant whisperings.

Here, indeed, was the fitting home of the evil Spirit of the hills, whose livid breath hovered ever over those grim spires that fanged into the high blue sky. Hatfield's eyes narrowed and little knots of muscle rippled along his lean jaw. He knew that Spirit of evil to be all too real and that in all earnestness it dwelt here in this tomb-like gloom, incarnate in the man whose maimed face was no more warped and distorted than his mental processes and his sense of ethical values. Hatfield felt cold at the thought of the possibility that the man's apparently wild words were true and that here in this grim gorge was one of Nature's storehouses of untold riches. With vast wealth at his command, what evil could not such a man do. Already the Ranger had viewed admitted specimens of his handiwork. The pitifully broken and agonized fragments of what had once been men were ample proof of utter ruthlessness and callous disregard of human suffering. Power in the hands of such a man was like those writhing flames which dwelt in the cavern abyss—devastating, all-consuming, indifferent to the destruction which followed their manifestations. A burning needle of pain in his left arm hammered home the truth in a horribly personal manner. For a moment, cold sweat started at his temples and his heart constricted as from the grip of an icy hand. Then his lean jaw tightened and his steady eyes turned coldly gray. The Lone Wolf did not permit personal considerations to come between him and duty.

His captors led him along the bank of the stream, in the shadow of the towering cliff. They passed a rough building, somewhat larger than the others, built solidly of timbers, its few narrow windows barred with heavy iron. Here, doubtless, the conscripted laborers were housed. A foul odor, as of death and corruption, drifted from the place as they passed.

"He doesn't take a chance by keeping 'em inside the cave when they aren't working," the Ranger reasoned. "Wonder where the guards hang out?"

No building that resembled a barracks for these last appeared. Hatfield decided that they dwelt in the cavern, which very likely provided chambers that could be made comfortable.

For fully a half mile the Ranger was led along the bank of the stream. The gorge was widening somewhat and clumps of stunted growth appeared. In the distance could be heard a growling murmur as of a waterfall, but if there were one, it was hidden by the discouraged-looking thickets.

The guards bore straight for one of these thickets and as they drew nearer, Hatfield saw a weatherbeaten cabin snugged amid the gnarled growth.

The cabin, solidly built of logs, with a massive stone chimney and a door of heavy planks, was undoubtedly much older than the other buildings he had observed. It appeared lonely and deserted and, when one of the guards unlocked a huge padlock and lifted a massive bar, the door swung open on hinges that creaked rustily. A moment later the Ranger was thrust into the single room and the door slammed shut again. He could hear the groan of the key in the big lock and the solid thump of the bar being jolted into place. Then the thud of departing footsteps.

For a moment, he could make out nothing in the intense gloom; then his eyes accustomed themselves to the wan light and he stared about.

There was a single window, devoid of glass and

strongly barred, through which he could see the guards vanishing back the way they had come. A bunk was built against one wall, ancient blankets tumbled upon it. There was a solidly constructed table and a single rough chair, both undoubtedly home-made. A few battered cooking utensils beside the stone fireplace completed the scanty furnishings.

Hatfield sat down on the bunk and fumbled in his pockets for "the makin's." He was surprised to find that only his gun had been taken. His other possessions, even his money, were intact. He could feel, snugged in a cunningly contrived and almost invisible pocket in his broad leather belt, the silver star set on a silver circle that was the badge of the Rangers. It had not been touched.

"Not that it means much," he mused. "That faceless jigger doesn't miss any bets. He knows I'm a Ranger: that's why he's so anxious to have me join him. He found killing me off wasn't a very easy job—muffed it three times. Then he got to thinking, and figured out that if he did kill me, it would mean another Ranger here in a hurry, maybe a troop. But a Ranger working under cover with him would simplify his problem. A few words from me to the right people would go a long way toward getting him what he wants, and I know just about what *that* is. Yes, a live Ranger in his loop would mean a lot. Smart, the way he went about it, too—never mentioned me being a Ranger; giving me an out for my conscience, I suppose. And when that failed—"

He did not finish the sentence, but his face grayed slightly as the stinging burn in his left arm manifested itself insistently. His lean jaw tightened and with a shrug of his wide shoulders he took up the problem more immediately to hand.

He thoughtfully smoked his cigarette, eying the room and its meager contents the while. The window he instantly disregarded as a possible avenue of escape. He doubted if it were large enough to get his shoulders through, even discounting the bars, which were massive and solidly imbedded in the timbers. The stone chimney he passed over for the same reason. The walls were of seasoned timbers, the floor of heavy planks hewn from logs with an axe. The roof was too high to be accessible and was solidly constructed. The door, strong as it appeared, he decided was the only possibility. Walking to it he shook it, lunged against it with a shoulder. It creaked slightly and that was all. He considered the chair and table as possible battering rams; the result was not hopeful. His gaze sought the fireplace and he was pleased to note that some of the heavy stones were loose.

After considerable effort he managed to dislodge one. With all his strength he hurled it against the door. A deep dent in the planks resulted, but the door held firm. He regarded it gloomily.

"I could pitch that rock at it all day and not get anywhere," he growled. "Wonder if there would be any chance of burning my way out of this shack?"

He discarded that idea, however. The chances of smothering to death were too good. Also, the smoke would certainly be seen at the cavern mouth.

Restlessly he pulled the blankets from the bunk. The bottom boards were heavy, with considerable spring to them, the kind usually chosen for bunk bases, being productive of greater comfort than more rigid planks. They were not nailed in but laid loosely on the frame. Hatfield lifted one from its bed and fingered the tough, springy wood. It was nearly seven feet long, an inch thick and about eight inches wide. Eyes brooding, he stared at it. His glance shifted to the door, took in the stone lying beside it. His eyes abruptly began to glow.

The floor boards were laid parallel to the door, and there were comparatively wide cracks between them. Hatfield managed to force the end of the board into a crack directly in front of and some ten feet distant from the door. He sighted over the upper end of it, his eyes glowing with excitement. He picked up the stone from the fireplace, turned it over in his slim hands, shook his head. His eyes roved about the room, fixed on the tumbled blankets. Folding one, he wrapped it around and around the board, a foot or so from the top, and knitted it firmly. The result was a little cloth "shelf," upon which he placed the stone; it lay secure. He had a rude but effective catapult.

Gripping the top of the board with both hands, he slowly pulled back on the springy wood. The tough plank bent more and more, creaking and groaning with the strain. The big muscles of the Ranger's back and shoulders writhed and bunched under his coat, his face tensed with effort. A last straining inch and he let go the board.

The tough plank sprang back, the stone whizzed through the air and struck the door with terrific force. One of the stout boards split from end to end.

Again the Ranger put his homely sling into operation; but his hand slipped and the stone whirled sideways, barely missing his arm. He shook his head at the mischance and tried again.

This time the stone flew straight and true, the door board split and splintered. One more smash of the big rock and it burst into shattered fragments. Hatfield wrenched the tough slivers free and jolted the cross bar from its brackets. The big lock still held firm but he had a narrow opening through which, after a great deal of squirming and effort, he was able to force his body.

For a moment he hesitated, glancing up the gorge toward where the cave mouth was located, then he turned and swiftly made his way in the opposite direction, keeping in the shadow of the cliff and as far away from the stream bank as possible.

As he walked, the growling murmur he had noticed before grew steadily louder. The floor of the gorge was very dusky now, the sun having slid toward the west and the slanting rays sent very little light into the depths. The roar was vibrating the air when the Ranger saw, rising before him, a glistening black wall. He muttered under his breath; it was as he had feared; the gorge was a box canyon and before him was the end wall.

At the base of the wall was a black opening into which the stream thundered. On either side were the frowning cliffs. A bristle of scanty, stunted growth straggled about the rocky floor of the gorge.

Hatfield paused uncertainly, turned and gazed back the way he had come. He looked at the black mouth into which the stream tumbled, and shook his head. Stepping back, he gazed up the almost perpendicular rise of the side wall, his eyes narrowing.

For as far as he could see, the rock was veined and mottled and crisscrossed with cracks and shattering ledges. Those precarious handholds might provide a way out of the gorge for a desperate man—a path fit to curdle the blood and still the heart, but a way. Death might well be waiting somewhere along that beetling stone face; but there was no doubt of the fate which awaited if he remained in the gorge to be run down and captured again by the devils who made it their dwelling place. The Lone Wolf's lean jaw set hard and his gray eyes glowed with resolve.

"Well, here goes!" he said aloud, and walked steadily to the base of the cliff.

For the first couple of hundred feet the ascent was comparatively simple. The ledges were broad and firm, the cracks in the stone wide and studded with hand and foot holds. Then the going swiftly grew more difficult. The stone face became less broken, the upward slant steeper. Hatfield shuffled back and forth in a tortuous zigzag, traveling long and exhausting distances to gain but a few upward feet. He was drenched with sweat, his hands were torn and bleeding, his legs numb with strain. He was forced to take longer and longer periods of rest where opportunity afforded.

One boon was granted him as he progressed upward: the light gradually grew stronger, silhouetting him against the darker face of the cliff but revealing holds that might have eluded him in the deeper shadows farther down. A feeling of confidence was growing within him; he was beginning to believe that he would actually make it to the top. And then—

Something buzzed through the air like an angry wasp and spatted against the stone only a few yards distant. Another angry buzz and his face was showered with stinging fragments of rock. To his ears came a sharp crack that flung back and forward between the rock walls in a myriad of shattering echoes.

Twisting about, he saw shadowy blotches racing down the gorge, and pale flickers of flame. His escape had been discovered!

CHAPTER XIV

A LONG crack, slanting steeply up the face of the cliff, appeared. Into this the fugitive slipped, climbing frantically. For the moment he was safe from the screeching slugs. The crack, made perhaps by a bolt of lightning, was hair-raisingly hazardous. The rock was shattered and crumbling. More than once knobs of stone gave way as the Ranger placed his weight upon them. Once he was left dangling by one hand, recovering only by a prodigious feat of strength. Once he had to stand on a narrow ledge and leap across and upward to a handhold beyond reach. For more than two hundred feet the crack pursued its zigzag way; then it petered out and the Ranger was again clinging like a fly to the surface of the wall.

A glance down showed a figure running swiftly back up the gorge.

"They only have sixguns, and the range is overlong," Hatfield quickly deduced. "He's hightailing it for a rifle. Well, I ought to be over the top before he gets back, if I'm ever going to get over."

The guns were still cracking in the gorge below, the echoes flinging back and forth between the walls, the bullets whining upward; but they were no longer much menace. The Ranger had gotten beyond the limit of effective pistol shooting. But a new and pressing danger presented itself.

Clinging to the face of the cliff several hundred feet below, but steadily drawing nearer, was a black smudge. One of the armed guards was climbing the cliff in pursuit of the fugitive; and Hatfield quickly realized that the fellow was an expert at the work; he was cover-

ing two feet of distance to the Ranger's one. Hatfield
turned his face to the cliff and redoubled his efforts.

To no avail. The pursuer was doubtless mountain
bred and thoroughly at home here, which the plainsman was not. Try as he would, the ominous shadow
closed the distance. Soon it would be in a position to
shoot the fugitive off the rock like a squirrel out of a
tree.

Ahead was a ledge, slanting upward at an easy angle.
It curved around a vast bulge in the cliff and vanished.
Hatfield made for it with all his strength. He had
almost reached it when the pursuer below tried his first
shot.

Hatfield felt the wind of the slug as it yelled past
him. A second bullet grazed his cheek, a third ripped
a hole in his coat sleeve. Then his feet reached the
ledge and he shuffled swiftly along it. A fourth bullet
knocked splinters in his face as he swung around the
bulge and out of range. A moment later he halted and
leaned panting against the cold rock.

The ledge came to an end a few yards from where he
stood. Here it was a good three feet in width, but
almost immediately it began to narrow, to sluff away
into nothing a little farther on. Above were knobs and
cracks and shatterings, over which the fugitive must
climb slowly and with care. In the meanwhile the
pursuer, standing secure on the ledge, would be able
to shoot him down at his ease.

For a moment Hatfield hesitated; then he turned and
grimly faced the bulge around which the ledge curved.
Tense, alert, he stood, every sense and every muscle
ready for a supreme effort.

For long minutes there was silence, then his straining
ears detected a faint shuffling that grew louder. Now
he could hear the panting breath of a laboring man.
Boots sounded the ledge. A sinewy, dark man swung
around the bulge.

Thrilled to heedlessness by the excitement of the
chase, he was totally unprepared for what awaited him.
But he was lightning fast and the flicker of his hand

to gun butt was as the rattler's stroke. Hatfield ducked under the gun that roared right in his face. He felt the heat of the discharge and heard the bullet scream over his shoulder. The next instant and he had closed with his pursuer and the two were fighting a battle to the death on the narrow ledge.

Hatfield's iron fingers had clamped the other's gun wrist and a terrific twist and jerk wrung the weapon from the other's hand. It fell to the ledge and was trampled over the edge by the straining, gasping combatants.

The man was shorter than Hatfield but he was broad of shoulder, deep of chest and his agility was bulwarked by immense strength. The sinewy fingers of his free hand bit deep into the Lone Wolf's throat. He levered a knee against the rock wall and desperately tried to swing the Ranger toward the edge of the narrow ledge. Madly the battlers strained and lunged, a thousand feet above the rocky floor of the gorge, the black loom of the cliff shooting up over them into the stainless blue sky.

A mighty lunge and one of Hatfield's feet went over the lip of the ledge. For a horrible instant he reeled and wavered with a thousand feet of nothing at all reaching up for his straining body. Then, by an almost superhuman effort, he regained his foothold and tore his throat free from the other's grasp. Letting go the wrist he leaped backward along the ledge. There was the gleam of a knife and the other rushed. Hatfield in one last desperate gamble dived headlong at the man's feet. His shoulder struck the other's ankles and he rolled over, poising on the very lip of the ledge, in his ears ringing a frightful scream of terror and despair that thinned away into the dark depths below.

Gasping and panting, shaking in every limb, the Ranger got slowly to his feet. He was alone on the ledge and that awful scream had stilled.

"Slammed him against the rock and bounced him over," he muttered, leaning over the edge and straining to pierce the shadows. The gloom was so deep now that he could see nothing save the tiny flash of an occasional pistol shot.

"You can't do any good with sixguns now," he growled, "but I'd better be moving before that fellow gets back with the rifle."

Resolutely he turned to the cliff and resumed the weary climb.

Every vein and crack and mottling of that last five hundred feet of cold rock remained stamped forever on the Ranger's memory. Giddy with fatigue, he clutched and scrambled his way upward, the broken rim above him seeming to grow no nearer. It actually did, however, and he was within fifty feet of it when the first rifle slug whined through the air.

It was nothing but guesswork shooting on the part of the unseen marksman, however, and only once did a bullet come dangerously close. It shattered a knob of stone almost under the Ranger's hand and the shock for a moment threw him perilously off balance. But just a little later his groping hand fastened on the firm, smooth stone of the rim and in an instant he had drawn his weary body over the lip and to safety. Below, the gorge was black with shadows, but here on the crest, the low lying sun shone brightly.

For a long time the Ranger lay stretched on the smooth rock, absorbing the warmth, too utterly tired to move. Finally he got stiffly to his feet and glanced about. A moment later he was trudging down a gentle incline that led to a bowl-like little valley stretching southward through the hills.

The valley curved slightly to the east and upon rounding a turn, Hatfield saw the secret of that mysterious cloud that seemed to hover like a Spirit of evil over the Tinaja Hills.

For half a mile or so were a succession of bubbling hot springs, of color-rimmed potholes from which jets of steam and hot water gushed at regular intervals. There were also fissures in the stone and from these trickled wisps of sulphurish smoke. From time to time Hatfield noticed unusual-appearing outcroppings of black or yellow material showing in the edges of seams and faults.

"Just like a little Yellowstone," the Ranger mused as he picked his way among these weird manisfestations of the eternal fires raging below. "Smells like hell," he added, his lips quirking in a wry grin, "and if that isn't hell I just came from, well—I don't want to go there!"

With a plainsman's sure instinct for direction, he bored through the hills as the sun sank behind the western crags and the shadows deepened. The moon came to his rescue before utter darkness shrouded the gorges and under its silvery light he reached the rangeland of the Regal ranch. He was some distance east of the grim gash in the earth that was Devil Canyon and dawn was graying the sky by the time he reached the southern wire. The sound of swift hoofs sent him into a thicket where the shadows were still deep.

Safely concealed, he watched two horsemen sweep out of the northwest. One he quickly identified as Don Sebastian Gomez. The other was his tall and swarthy attendant whose scarred face bore the marks of Yaqui knives.

The Lone Wolf stared after them with brooding eyes as they vanished in the direction of the Regal ranchhouse. His mind shifted backward and forward over the events of the past twenty-four hours.

"I don't know all the tie-ups—yet, or what it's all about," he mused, "but I do know who that faceless fiend is!"

Chapter XV

"You're a sight!"

Old Hogface Holliday stared at the Ranger in amazement. With the sun of mid-morning pouring through
the window of the little back room and showing up
every detail, Hatfield did present an appearance worthy
of comment.

"What happened to yuh?" Hogface added.

"Horse fell," Hatfield replied cryptically. Hogface
continued to stare.

"Yeah? Musta fell inter Devil Canyon, for the
looks of yuh!"

Hatfield glanced at him quickly. "Devil Canyon?
What's that?"

"It's that devil-claw mark what runs across the Regal
range and on up inter the hills," Hogface explained.

"What's in it?" Hatfield asked.

"Rock and bad water and scrub and thorns," Hogface replied. "Leastwise so much as anybody knows.
Nobody ever goes down there."

"Nobody?"

"Well, nobody for a almighty long time, anyhow. I
never heerd tell of but one feller goin' down there, and
he never was seed no more."

"Who was he?"

"Fool prospector by the name of Paxton. Happened
'bout ten years back, best I rec'lect. He let hisself down
inter that gully by a rope. Let his pack down fust and
slid after it. Had a Injun feller waitin' up top for
him. Injun hung 'round a coupla days and then come
to town. Some fellers rode out to see 'bout it and one
of 'em climbed down the rope a ways. Saw there

weren't nothin' but fast runnin' water underneath. Wasn't hard to figger that Paxton fell inter that water and got drowned. Anyhow, he never come back. Was a fine big goodlookin' black-eyed feller. Eddicated, too. Usta spend a lot of time over to Doc Austin's office; Doc's got a considerable library. Paxton usta read a lot in it when he wasn't prospectin' up in the hills. That was when folks figgered there was gold or somethin' val'ble in them hills. They been purty well looked over now and nothin' int'restin' ever been located but some hot springs and sulphur water up near the head of Devil Canyon. Canyon's almighty deep up there. Ain't much over a hundred foot to the bottom down thisaway, but the bottom's all brush and rock and stuff and the sides overhang so's yuh can't see anythin' much."

"You say it was ten years ago that Paxton went into the canyon?"

"Thereabouts. Wasn't so very long 'fore Sebastian Gomez come up from Mexico and bought the place from John Wentworth. Yeah, it was all of ten years back. But, say! What we standin' here gabbin' for? You need washin' up and some doctorin' for them hands. Yuh say yuh got another pair of britches and a clean shirt in yore saddlebags? I'll take yore coat and have my Mexican fix it up; he's good at that kind of thing."

He glanced shrewdly at Hatfield as the latter doffed the garment and handed it to him.

"Reckon yuh got this round hole in the sleeve when yore hoss fell, eh?" he remarked sarcastically.

"Funny things happen sometimes when horses fall," Hatfield replied. Hogface nodded his white head.

"Yeah, so I've heerd tell," he commented dryly. "Hustle up, now, and get cleaned up. It's way past time to eat."

In the privacy of the little room above the saloon, Hatfield undid the bandage and examined his left arm. The wound, which looked like the rasp made by a file, was already slightly inflamed and a dull throbbing was discernible. The flesh of the upper arm was a trifle swollen. The Lone Wolf's eyes grew coldly gray as he gazed at it and his lips set in a hard line. The eyes were calm and his face devoid of emotion, however, when he later descended to the back room, after making good use of the plentiful supply of hot water brought him by a wrangler. Hogface was already seated at the table.

"Come on," he exclaimed, "let's eat. I got somethin' to tell yuh.

"There's a big game on fer t'night," he explained over the dishes. "Old Anse McCoy'll be here and Cartwright and Boyles and Tracy and Don Sebastian Gomez. That's the only time them two ever get t'gether decent. They're both crazy 'bout poker and both are bangup players. This is the fust time they've played since the shootin' 'tween their outfits, but they've both sent word they're comin'. Their men won't mix, but they'll b'have themselves while their bosses is playin' poker. Funny thing, ain't it, how two fellers what plumb hate each other can get t'gether over somethin' they're both a lot int'rested in? I've knowed it to happen that way lots of times with lots of fellers."

Hatfield nodded, and in his steady gray eyes was a sudden warm glow.

"Yes," he replied, "sometimes you can get men who think they hate each other t'gether and hold 'em that way with something they're both interested in, particularly if they happen to be good fellows at bottom."

"I allus figgered that Gomez and McCoy was both sorta good fellers at bottom," Hogface grunted over his fifth cup of coffee, "but Devil Anse shore manages to keep his goodness well covered up!"

Hatfield slept the rest of the day and awoke refreshed, save for a growing soreness in his left arm. His eyes were somber when he descended to the saloon, but he evinced no signs of apprehension as he took his place at the big table in the corner.

It was still early, but the saloon was filling. The Ranger noted a festive air and one of expectancy. Word of the big game pending had gotten about. A game in which Sebastian Gomez and Devil Anse McCoy took part was always productive of interest, he gathered. Now, when an open break between the rival outfits had already occurred and a bitter range war was in the making, the interest was intensified. Men who had not been in town for weeks were appearing. Several dark-faced haciendados from below the line put in an appearance, and a couple of big mine owners from the left bank of the Rio Grande, attracted by the high stakes in prospect.

Sheriff Dent Crane appeared, a worried look on his face. Beside him sauntered Highpockets Hilton, his taciturn deputy, hiding behind a grin as usual, but with little of mirth in his twinkling eyes. Crane walked over and engaged Hatfield in conversation.

"I'm dependin' on you to help keep peace 'tween them two old hellions," he said. "A good dealer can do a lot if he's a mind to. If a row should happen to start, no knowing where it'll end. There'll be Gomez men and McCoy men, plenty of both, in this room t'night, and they'll be loaded for bear."

He glanced around and swore gloomily.

"I don't see why they didn't send some Rangers over here like I asked for," he complained.

Highpockets Hilton was staring thoughtfully at Jim Hatfield. He fingered his houn' dawg chops and nodded to himself, almost in the manner of one who makes an important discovery.

"Rangers," he announced to nobody in particular, "is like gold."

"What yuh mean by that?" demanded Sheriff Crane.

"Because," replied Highpockets, grinning at Hatfield in a friendly fashion, "Rangers is where yuh find 'em!"

A little later the Bar M outfit arrived. Hobbling into the saloon at their head came old Anse McCoy, a wizened figure in a shabby black coat, his filmy little eyes snapping and glittering, his toothless jaws working spasmodically on a cud of "eatin' terbaccer." Behind him filed Sid McCoy, his handsome grandson, face still somewhat bruised and discolored, Chet

Madison, his surly foreman, and others of the Bar M riders. Nigger Mike Brocas was not among those present. He was doubtless still nursing his wounded shoulder.

Old Anse took a seat at the table and glared appraisingly at Hatfield. Apparently satisfied, he worried off another "chaw," took deadly aim at a fly on the rim of a cuspidor eleven feet distant and sent a stream of amber juice, and the fly, into the dark interior of the gaboon.

The Bar M riders lined the bar and downed straight whisky. A couple of cattlemen and two mine owners drew up chairs and Hatfield called for cards. While he was stripping the cover from a deck, Don Sebastian Gomez and his vaqueros put in an appearance. Hatfield was surprised to see that his red-haired granddaughter, Karen Walters, accompanied him. She took a seat at a table near the orchestra and old Hogface Holliday bustled over to join her. She greeted him in a friendly fashion and as Don Sebastian drew up the remaining chair at the poker table, she suddenly rose to her feet and walked gracefully across the room to pause beside Jim Hatfield's chair. She looked him frankly in the eyes and held out her hand.

"I'm sorry for what I did the other day," she said. "I didn't understand."

Hatfield rose to his feet, removed his black hat and smiled down at her from his great height. His strangely colored eyes were suddenly all kindness and his stern face wonderfully pleasant to look upon.

"Don't ever be afraid to do what you think's right, little lady," he said in his deep voice, "and you have the right idea in not being afraid to say so when you make a mistake. Keep that in mind about ten minutes from now."

The girl stared at him wonderingly, but he only smiled again, squeezed her firm little hand gently and sat down. She hesitated a moment and went back to her table. From the corner of his eye, Hatfield saw Sid

McCoy leave the bar and saunter around the room with elaborate unconcern. It took him some little while to reach the table near the orchestra. With a nod to Hogface he drew up a vacant chair and began asking the saloonkeeper questions.

Karen Walters stared at him with hostile eyes; then suddenly her glance was irresistibly drawn to the poker table across the way. Jim Hatfield, expertly riffling the cards with his slim fingers, was smiling at her and his gray eyes were sunny as summer seas. Karen blushed with sudden understanding and turned back to her own table. A little later, Hatfield noted that she had joined in the conversation, and that Sid McCoy was fast losing his interest in Hogface Holliday's remarks. Neither Don Sebastian nor Devil Anse had noticed this bit of byplay.

Old Anse had favored Don Sebastian with a watery glare when the *hidalgo* took his seat and Don Sebastian had returned it with a look of cool hostility. After that neither appeared to pay any attention to the other.

The play was steep and as the night wore on it grew steeper. Shortly after midnight the two cattlemen, Tracy and Boyles, shoved back their chairs. The two miners were not long in following suit. Old Anse and Don Sebastian, tall stacks of yellow chips before them, hunched low over their cards. Men who had been watching the play drew nearer. The Bar M waddies and the Lazy R vaqueros had long since left the bar and were absorbed in the game.

Back and forth seesawed the game, and by the minute old Anse grew more viciously angry, Don Sebastian more coldly hostile. Up to the present, neither had spoken a direct word to the other. Suddenly Devil Anse slammed a discarded hand on the table.

"Gomez," he rasped, leaning forward, his jaws champing, his rheumy eyes snapping, "this is jest a waste of time. Air ye a gambler, or ain't ye?"

Don Sebastian stared coldly. "I do not think you need to ask that question," he replied.

"All right," rasped Devil Anse, "we're admittin' ye

air. So here's a gamble for ye. I done callated for some time this state ain't big 'nough to hold the both of us. I'll play ye my spread 'gainst yores, the loser to get outa the country. One hand of stud poker. Air ye game?"

A low murmur swept the room. The Bar M waddies and the Lazy R vaqueros stiffened, leaned closer. Men seemed to hold their breath as they awaited Don Sebastian's reply.

Jim Hatfield stole a quick glance at the table near the orchestra. Sid McCoy was staring at the poker table, a strange light in his eyes. The girl was white to the lips. Instinctively her glance sought the man at her side. Don Sebastian's voice brought Hatfield's attention back to the business at hand.

"It is a mad thing to do, but I will take your wager," he said quietly.

Devil Anse laughed creakily. "New deck of cyhads!" he called. "Deal 'em slow and easy, son, slow and easy."

A man who had been unobtrusively watching the game, a tall man with sombrero drawn low and his face hidden almost to the eyes by his muffling serape, suddenly turned and sauntered to the bar. While Hatfield was preparing the new deck, he spoke softly to several swarthy men grouped there and then vanished through the swinging doors into the night. The men at the bar drew closer together.

The room was deathly silent as Hatfield dealt each player a hole card, face down. Gomez and McCoy carefully raised a corner and peeked, faces expressionless. Slowly and deliberately, Hatfield dealt each a second card, face upward. Gomez caught a ten-spot, McCoy a king. A long sigh went up from the silent watchers. On the third deal, Don Sebastian drew a deuce of hearts, old Anse a four of spades. There was a nervous shifting of feet, and glares from those disturbed by the sound. Nerves were strained to the breaking point. The fourth card came slowly from the deck—a nine-spot of diamonds for Devil Anse, a king of clubs for Don Sebastian. A murmur like a wind in wet trees ran through the room. Four cards out and no pairs in sight! Hatfield's slim fingers reached toward the deck and the fifth and last card.

With the appalling abruptness of a thunderclap, a fight started at the bar. There was a shot and a yell, the gleam of a knife. A knot of swarthy men, cursing, kicking, striking, whirled through the crowd. They slammed into the poker table like a herd of bucking steers. Over it went, cards, chips, players and chairs. Hatfield alone escaped the general downfall, surging catlike from his chair and reeling back against the wall.

Through the howling crowd spun the battlers, and out the swinging doors. Shots and yells sounded outside the saloon, then the clatter of fast hoofs beating away into the distance.

Inside the First Chance was a madhouse. Men were howling, screaming, cursing. Devil Anse McCoy scrambled to his feet, his cane clattering, and shook his fist under Don Sebastian's nose.

"Ye blankety-blank-blank blankety-blank!" he howled, "ye had that done a-purpose! Them was greasers staged that fake row! Yuh know I had yuh beat and did it to save yore wuthless skin. I had an ace in the hole, blankety-blank-blank you."

"Silence!" roared Don Sebastian, shaken for once out of his habitual calm. "I too had an ace in the hole and my ten-spot was higher than your nine!"

Chet Madison leaped to the front. "That's a likely soundin' yarn!" he bawled. "Why, yuh—"

Pedro Zorrila, Don Sebastian's scarred foreman, dived for Chet, knife gleaming. Madison went for his gun.

Like a leaping catamount, Jim Hatfield went into action. He knocked Pedro heels-over-head with a backward slap, gripped Chet Madison by the shoulders and slammed him into a chair.

"Sit down!" he roared at the Bar M foreman.

There is a psychological something that puts a seated man at more than a mere physical disadvantage. Chet gulped and goggled. The surging Bar M and Lazy R hands hesitated for a fatal instant.

Bowling men over like ninepins came Sheriff Dent Crane and Highpockets Hilton. Both held cocked sawed-off shotguns. After them came Hogface Holliday and his bartenders, likewise armed. Before these yawning muzzles of death and destruction, the crowd shrank back. The sheriff's voice blared at them—

"This'll be all for t'night! Yuh're not goin' to tear this town to pieces for a while yet. Gomez, you and yore men fork yore cayuses and get outa town, pronto. McCoy, yore outfit is stayin' right here for half a hour. No arg'fyin', now. My trigger finger's gettin' itchy. If there's got to be a range war 'round here t'night, I'll be the one what starts it!"

With menacing eyes and compressed lips, the Lazy R vaqueros left the saloon. The Bar M waddies returned the glares with interest. Jim Hatfield noticed, however, that when Karen Walters said goodbye to Sid McCoy she did not glare. The Lone Wolf's firm lips quirked in a grin as he turned to find Highpockets Hilton's twinkling eyes upon him.

"Yeah," chuckled Highpockets with a sociable wink, "Rangers is shore like gold!"

As Hatfield made his way to the back room, a bartender stopped him and handed him a folded bit of paper.

"Mexican lookin' feller with a blanket wrapped 'round his face told me to give yuh this," said the drink juggler. "He slipped out 'fore I could ask him who it was from."

Hatfield unfolded the paper. On it were written four words in heavy black letters—

YOUR TIME IS SHORT

He stared at the ominous black lettering for a moment, then carefully placed the paper in a safe pocket.

With a shrug of his broad shoulders he strove to dismiss the warning. But all the while, the steady throb in his left arm kept beating in rhythmical cadence—"Your time is short! Your time is short!"

CHAPTER XVI

WHEN Hatfield visited Bandy Burton's livery stable the following morning, a surprise awaited him.

"I came to pay you for that horse," he told the ex-cowboy.

"What hoss?" demanded Bandy.

"The horse you rented me," Hatfield replied. "He—"

The words suddenly died on his lips, for Bandy was pointing to a nearby stall. From the stall rose a familiar bay head.

"Where in blazes did you find him?" Hatfield wondered.

"Feller rode him inter town this mawnin'," explained Bandy. "Said he found him runnin' loose on the range. Was sorta put out when I showed him my bill of sale describin' the cayuse and ridin' outfit, but he didn't do no arg'fyin'. I give him a coupla dollars for bringin' him in."

Hatfield passed Bandy a gold piece. "Guess this'll square everything," he said. "Who was the fellow who brought him in?"

"Mexican feller—rides for Don Sebastian Gomez of the Regal ranch."

From the livery stable, Hatfield went to Doc Austin's office. The old physician received him cordially.

"Shore yuh can look over my library," said Doc. "Glad to have yuh do it. Ain't many fellas hereabouts what 'preciate books. Anythin' pertickler yuh'd like to look at? Help yoreself."

He watched Hatfield select several volumes on mineralogy and metallurgy. He chuckled as the Ranger began turning the well-thumbed pages.

"Funny thing," said Doc. "Yuh're the fust feller in ten years what's looked at them books. Feller usta come in 'bout that time ago and read outa them works. He usta mark notes on the margins of the pages. Callate some of them notes is there still. Yeah, there's one right now."

For long minutes Hatfield stared at the notations penciled on the margin of a yellow leaf.

"Feller by the name of Pax—Baxter—nope, that wasn't it. It was, let's see. Oh, yeah, Paxton, that was it. He was a minin' feller and was all time browsin' 'round up in the hills lookin' for gold or somethin'. Took a fool notion to go down inter Devil Canyon. Never come back. Usta have a Injun tracker with him when he went inter the hills. By gum! I jest rec'lect! That blankety-blank Patchy yuh plugged through the shoulder was the Injun. He sorta drapped outa sight after Paxton got lost in the canyon. Coupla years back he showed up 'round here and went to work for Anse McCoy. A gambler and allus seems to have plenty of money. Callate that's one reason Anse hired him, 'cause he's sich a good poker player. Anse swears by anyone who can play good poker, that is 'ceptin' Sebastian Gomez. He swears at him! Hear tell Anse give Nigger Mike reg'lar blue blazin' hell for that mixup he got inter with you. Anse don't go in for no crooked work where cards is consarned. Funny thing, ain't it, I'd rec'lect to connect Nigger Mike with Paxton when we started talkin' of him. I'd plumb forgot to think of the two t'gether. Pore Paxton, he was a fine lookin' feller and one of the strongest men I ever seed. Could straighten a hoss shoe with his bare hands."

While the garrulous old doctor ran on, Hatfield was listening with one attentive ear and turning the leaves of the book on mineralogy at the same time. Several items interested him greatly and as he read—

    . . . larger ore bodies are associated with massive

> beds of sandstone . . . seams of greenish shale less than two feet thick underlie the ore and appear in places to have influenced its deposition . . . cylindrical masses commonly called "trees" or "logs" . . . surface indication . . . material showing in the edges of seams and faults . . .

—his eyes glowed dark and the concentration furrow between his black brows deepened.

After an hour or more he closed the volume, but just before doing so, he did a strange thing for an evident book lover to do: he carefully removed a page, folded it, and slipped it into his pocket. He glanced through a second book dealing with similar subjects, and then took from the shelf a thin volume of fresher appearance than the former two.

"That's a translation from a French work," Doc Austin offered. "I've found it almighty int'restin'. That stuff they're talkin' 'bout in there is sure bein' a help to sufferin' humanity, and they don't half know yet what all it's good for. A pity there ain't more of it to be had. The woman they tell 'bout in there is shore some little lady, all right."

The book was the story of Marie Curie and her husband and their discovery of radium.

"That's it!" Hatfield exulted. "Emanations from radium would do just what happened to those Mexicans and Tom Hardy, and to that faceless fiend!"

Fragmentary sentences of what he had just read recurred to him—

> . . . over-exposure or too frequent exposure to powerful radiation may induce a severe ulcerative process, which will endanger life and require the most skilled surgical intervention before a possible cure can be affected . . . loss of hair, blindness, followed later by death . . . paresis, ataxia, and convulsions, followed later by death . . .

"Sure death unless somebody knows the cure," he

mused, thumbing the pages of the book, "and it appears nobody knows a cure, unless that faceless fiend happened to be telling the truth. Maybe he was. Anyhow, down in that hole, he and the man he's working with have got about the richest deposit of carnotite ore in the world, and carnotite's the chief source of radium."

He settled himself comfortably in the chair, rested his sore left arm on the table and gave his entire attention to the book.

Until the afternoon shadows were long, Jim Hatfield sat absorbed in the story of sacrifice, heroic endeavor, suffering, and epic discovery. When at last he turned the final page, it was with a sigh of regret. He stood up, flexed his long arms, keenly conscious of the soreness and slight stiffness of the left one, and smiled down at the little old doctor who was nodding in his chair.

"Yes," he said softly, "there are plenty of fine folks in the world to balance up for the bad ones."

His eyes were coldly gray as he gazed toward the grim hills to the north.

"Just about tied up," he mused, "all but one or two little things, and we'll fix the knots in them, pronto."

Thanking the old doctor for the use of his books, he left the office and returned to the livery stable. Dusk was falling, but he saddled his big sorrel and headed for the railroad town twenty miles to the west. There he sent a long telegram to Captain Bill McDowell at the Franklin Ranger Post. Then he rode back to Vegas and went to bed.

It was raining when Hatfield awoke, a thin, misty rain with an unpleasant chill to it, a chill that did not tend to make his sore left arm feel any better. Examination showed that a foul looking pustule was forming where the wound had been. He carefully bandaged it and went down stairs for breakfast. Night was falling when he returned to his room.

Swiftly he changed clothes, a well-worn cowboy outfit coming out of his capacious saddlebags to replace the black coat and white shirt. He cuffed a crumpled "J.B." into shape and tilted its wide brim over one eye. Heavy double cartridge belts encircled his slim waist, the black guns sagging low in their carefully worked and oiled cut-out holsters. It was the Lone Wolf who left the saloon by the back door and made his way to the little livery stable. Bandy Burton eyed the metamorphosis with no surprise.

"Callate yuh'd get tired of them gambler duds and go back to the clothes yuh're usta wearin'," was his only comment. "What hoss yuh ridin'?"

Hatfield grinned and reached for his heavy Mexican saddle. The tall sorrel nipped playfully at his ear and stamped in his stall. Swiftly the Ranger cinched the big saddle, adjusted the stirrup straps slightly and turned to Bandy.

"I need a rope," he said, "about a hundred-footer, good and strong."

"Can let yuh have a coupla sixty-footers," the little ex-puncher replied, "good twine. Yuh can splice 'em t'gether."

"That'll be fine," the Ranger replied. "Now will you take a note to Highpockets Hilton for me?"

Bandy nodded. "Glad to. Anythin' else?"

Hatfield was tying some small parcels into a compact bundle which he stowed in one of his saddlebags.

"No, don't think there is," he replied. He wrote a few words on a bit of paper while the stableman was procuring the rope. He folded the small sheet and handed it to Bandy. Leading the sorrel to the door he swung into the saddle with lithe grace.

"Good luck, hope yuh get 'em," the little ex-cowboy called as Goldy danced away, exulting in the chance to stretch his long legs after a period of inactivity.

Hatfield grinned over his shoulder and waved a hand to the little man.

"You can cover up where some folks are concerned, but it's no use with others," he confided to the sorrel, thinking of Highpockets Hilton's sociable wink. Goldy snorted and lengthened his stride.

In the course of one of their talks, Hogface Holliday had accurately located Devil Canyon for the Ranger.

Hatfield took down a section of wire, entered the Regal enclosure and rode north until he reached the end of the box. He followed the right rim of the canyon for some little distance, finally coming upon a spot that fitted into his plans.

Through a dense thicket of chaparral a little spring gushed from under a rock and sent a feathery plume of water spraying into the canyon. The thicket was so dense that Goldy forced himself through with great difficulty and was well scratched and in a thoroughly bad temper when he finally reached a little semicircular clearing on the very lip of the canyon. He was somewhat mollified when Hatfield removed saddle and bridle and gave him an opportunity to roll on the thick grass that carpeted the clearing. He watched with a dubious eye while the Ranger kindled a fire about the size of a plate and deftly boiled coffee and fried bacon and eggs taken from his saddlebags.

After the meal was eaten and the dishes washed and stored away, Hatfield rolled up in his blanket and went to sleep. Goldy cropped grass, dozed and otherwise tranquilly enjoyed himself until the first rose and gold of dawn streaked the graying sky. He pricked his ears expectantly as Hatfield awoke; but the Ranger did not saddle up after eating his breakfast. Instead he smoked a leisurely cigarette and then sauntered to the rim of the canyon and gazed earnestly into the dark depths.

Even in the freshening light of morning, little was to be seen other than the slightly waving tops of gnarled little trees, clumps of black rock and an occasional glint of water. Hatfield measured the distance to the rocks below and nodded his satisfaction.

Sturdy burr oaks grew close to the canyon's edge where the curving line of the growth snugged the clearing. To one of these Hatfield fastened the end of the light but strong rope provided by Bandy Burton. The more than a hundred feet length of line dangled down the face of the canyon wall, looking scantly more substantial than a bit of pack thread. Hatfield made a bundle of what was left of the cooked bacon and fried dough cake he had had for breakfast and slung it about his shoulder.

"You stay here and behave yourself till I come back," he told the sorrel. "You have plenty to eat and lots of water. Now don't go raising trouble and let somebody find out you're here."

Goldy cocked an attentive ear, snorted contempt for such unnecessary admonition and went back to cropping grass. Hatfield gave the rope a final tentative pull, slipped over the edge and went down hand over hand.

The cliff bulged and before he reached bottom he found he was overhanging the swift water, with a narrow strip of bank ten feet distant. He calculated the distance and began to swing his body back and forth. Wider and wider grew the arc he described. Finally, at the inner extreme of the swing he let go and dropped lightly to the ground. The rope swung back to hang well out of reach, but a long branch with a projecting limb cut short would remedy that. Hatfield hitched his gunbelt a little higher and headed up the canyon, keeping under cover of the thick growth as much as possible.

It was a wearisome trudge, for the canyon floor was rough and rocky and the growth impeded progress. From time to time he caught glimpses of the dark rock of the wall, but for the most time the screen of leaves and branches hid it from view. Once or twice he noted the dark yawn of cavern mouths. These interested him greatly, but he did not care to risk investigating them at the moment. The sun climbed the long slant of the eastern sky, hung directly overhead, for a moment a coppery disc with radiations of pale gold, and then reeled westward.

Gloomier and gloomier grew the canyon as the walls increased in height. The vegetation took on a dank, unhealthy look. From time to time the Ranger heard stealthy rustlings and once the buzz of a rattlesnake, strident, threatening, told that venomous life at least had its being in these sunless depths.

The gloom was intense when the Ranger's uncanny instinct for distance and direction told him that he was nearing his goal. He heard a shout, startlingly near, and the click of boot heels on rock. A little later he cautiously parted a fringe of growth and stared at a black cavern mouth and a cluster of rude buildings.

A line of men were shuffling from the cavern—men whose legs dragged woodenly and whose shoulders had a hopeless sag. Even at that distance, the Ranger could see evidence of the ravages of terrible affliction. His eyes grew frosty at the sight and his lean jaw tightened.

Beside the line walked armed guards, alert, erect. Hatfield counted more than a dozen. Some were Yaquis or Mexican-Yaquis. Others were not.

The line of shambling laborers was marched to the rambling building with the barred windows. Hatfield heard the heavy door slam and the rattle of a key. The guards reentered the cavern mouth. Cooking smells wafted about. The Ranger opened his packet of dough cake and bacon, munched contentedly and washed it down with cold water from the stream. He wished for a cigarette, but the risk was too great.

Denser and denser grew the gloom. Far overhead, a streak of blue sky still shone brightly, but on the canyon floor was only darkness and the murmur of the waters.

There was activity about the cave mouth, however. Lights flickered, men came and went. Hatfield could see the glowing ends of cigarettes. Voices arose in a queer hodge-podge of languages. There was a clink of glass. Once the Ranger saw a tall blanketed form outlined in a beam of light. He thought it was the faceless man, but could not be sure. Stars were sprinkling the high strip of sky now, and a faint glow of moonlight.

Hours passed, and finally the activity at the cave mouth lessened and died. Lights flickered up the long corridor, grew small and vanished. Darkness and silence followed, broken only by the murmur of the water and a low throb that welled from the cave mouth, the tireless voice of the rushing fires within.

Still the Ranger lay quietly in his place of concealment. Not until the dead hour that precedes the dawn did he steal cautiously from the growth. He passed the squat little dynamite building that perched precariously on the bank of the stream, slipped down the path and approached the mouth of the cave. In the almost total dark it seemed to glow palely and take on the semblance of grinning skeleton jaws sagging loosely. A moment later those sinister jaws of death swallowed his tall form.

Chapter **XVII**

SILENTLY as a purposeful ghost, the Ranger stole along the black corridor. Outside, the stone seemed slightly luminous with the stored up dregs of dead light, but here the darkness was absolute. Not until the roar of the subterranean fires was trembling the air and the heat was beating out in pulsing waves did the walls of the corridor become dimly visible. A moment later he crouched against the wall close to the entrance of the great inner cave and studied the ominous scene.

Lonely and deserted was the lofty room now, with no sign of life, and no movement other than the writhing and swirling of the tall columns of burning gas. The jets under the crucibles had been extinguished, apparently by the simple means of shoving a thick block of stone over the vents in the cavern floor. No straining, tortured figures stirred with the iron ladles or bent beneath the sacks of heavy ore. No brown or yellow faced guards stood watching with ready rifles. But the massive beds of sandstone were the same and those strange veins of yellow or sable ore with their basing of greenish shale.

Hatfield nodded with satisfaction. "Yes, that's it," he mused, "plate-like masses and lenses and cylindrical masses. But these are thicker and longer and richer looking than anything the books told about. There probably isn't another deposit like this in the world. Talk about the seven cities of Cibola that Coronado looked for! If they'd been as full of gold as he believed, they wouldn't have been a patch on this!"

Silently he turned and made his way back along the corridor, very slowly, very carefully, his fingertips continually brushing the righthand wall. He paused when they contacted the rough planks of a wooden door.

"That'll be the laboratory place I was in," he muttered. "Now let's see, it ought to be about fifty paces farther along."

At approximately the distance he estimated, his search was rewarded. His fingers brushed the second wooden door, the one his guards had instinctively edged away from as they led him from the corridor to imprison him in the old cabin. Carefully he felt it over from top to bottom, discovered the hasp and the clumsy padlock that held it in place. He fumbled the lock for a moment, drew one of his guns and thrust the heavy barrel through the shackle. A couple of wrenches and there was a sharp crack as the brittle iron of the shackle snapped. The lock fell to the ground with a soft little clang.

For long minutes the Ranger listened intently, gun ready for instant action. There was no sound save the rushing murmur of the fire. Gently he lifted the hasp from the staple and shoved open the door. He entered the dark, silent room and closed the door behind him.

Dark? Not quite. A faint, spontaneously luminous glow seemed to permeate the gloom. Apparently suspended in the night, gleamed phosphorescent bluish outlines. Pale, shimmering, mysterious sources of radiation, like to a fairy setting of glowworms. There was something ghostly and beautiful about this necklace of fire gems set about the ebon throat of the darkness. Hatfield breathed deeply as he gazed upon it, and in his heart was a swelling exultation.

"I didn't tangle my rope that time," he mused under his breath. "Made a perfect throw and no fooling. Here it is—just as I thought."

Cautiously he struck a match. The tiny flame lighted a small chamber carved in the living rock. Around the walls were racks in which were placed tiny glass receivers. They winked dully in the flicker of the match, but the instant the flame died, the fairy fireflies leaped into being once more.

Hatfield shook his head as he moved toward the door. He apostrophised the faceless man—

"Just like the tramp who found the thousand-dollar bill! He was rich, but it didn't do him a bit of good. He couldn't spend it and if he tried to get it changed, he'd have to explain where he got it and then the one who really owned it would show up and take it away from him. That's the way with this man: he's got it, but if he tries to do anything with it, he'll have to explain where he got it; and he can't explain, yet. No wonder he's scheming and conniving. And has he got to be stopped! Well, he will be!"

His eyes were cold as the breath from a winter waterfall and his usually good-humored mouth was a hard and merciless line as he stepped through the door and closed it after him. Again he apostrophised the faceless man—

"You had your chance. You found some way to cure yourself before it finished you. You could have cured those other poor devils, if you'd been anything but a sidewinder. You didn't! Yes, you had your chance, and muffed it!"

He fitted the broken lock back into place as best he could. It might pass the inspection of a casual glance.

"There will be plenty of trouble when it's found out," he chuckled soundlessly, "but finding out how it was broken will be something else again."

The strip of sky was brightening with dawn when he slipped back into his place of concealment amid the growth. Half of his task was successfully consummated. The other and more dangerous half was yet to come.

"Yes, I've got to find out how they get in and out of this hole," he muttered. "They don't slide down a rope, that's certain. There's a way out, all right, one that horses can take, I think, but the chances are I could hunt for a year without stumbling on it except by plain luck, and I can't depend too much on luck."

Burrowing deep in the sheltering growth, he curled up and went to sleep. Sounds at the cave mouth awakened him several hours later. The guards were herding the shambling laborers into the gloomy corridor. The muscles rippled along Hatfield's lean jaw as he gazed on the hopeless faces, many of them scarred and ravished, and the filmy, lack-lustre eyes. He could almost vision the bony hand of death that reached for each bowed shoulder—the death that would be their only surcease from suffering. He moved slightly to ease the position of his dully throbbing left arm.

The last of the guards vanished inside the corridor. Hatfield ate the remainder of his bread and bacon, drank deeply from the stream and settled down to watch. A new sound brought his head around with a snap. He writhed toward the stream, parted a screen of branches and stared silently.

"So that's how they travel!" he muttered. "I might have known it!"

The sound had been the click of oars in rowlocks. Moving diagonally down the stream was an unwieldy looking boat. There were five men in the boat. Two were rowing and two were keeping watch on a fifth man, who was evidently a prisoner. As the boat was brought to the bank near the dynamite shack and the captive shoved ashore, Hatfield exclaimed sharply under his breath. The man, staggering slightly, blood on his face, but with defiant head held high, was Sid McCoy!

Chapter XVIII

Tensely Hatfield watched the guards herd their prisoner ashore. Two, prodding him with gun muzzles, marched him to the long shack which housed the laborers. The remaining two, after securing the boat, sauntered into the cave mouth and vanished. A little later one man followed them from the shack. The other had evidently remained to keep an eye on the prisoner.

For long minutes Jim Hatfield lay motionless, thinking furiously, endeavoring to revise his plans to accord with this unexpected development.

"I don't dare take a chance on leaving him with them," he muttered apropos of Sid McCoy. "The devil only knows what they're liable to do to him. He's a hot-headed jigger and he'll be sure to do something to stir up those sidewinders, and they don't need riling anyhow to get them on the prod. No, I can't take the chance."

Slowly, stealthily, cursing the mischance that was liable to cause all his well-laid plans to miscarry, he moved along the stream in the direction of the long shack.

There were dangerously open spaces to be covered and Hatfield held his breath as he negotiated them. Near the shack the growth was thick, however, and he was within a few yards of the building when he peered through a final fringe and saw the guard leaning idly against a corner, smoking a cigarette. The man's back was to him and his pose showed no thought of danger.

Like a drifting smoke wraith, Hatfield covered the distance. His hands were reaching for the guard's neck when he stepped on a dry stick that broke under his

125

foot with a sharp crack. The guard turned, his jaw sagged in utter amazement and for a split second he stood paralyzed. And in that tense moment, death leaped at him. Too late he clawed madly for his gun and his mouth opened to yell.

Fingers like rods of nickel steel closed on his throat. The Ranger's other hand gripped the darting gun wrist. An instant of furious struggle and the man was whirled into the air. His body hit the rocky ground with a crunching thud. He groaned softly once, sagged like a bundle of old clothes and lay still. Hatfield swiftly went through his pockets, found a large key and fitted it into the lock that secured the door of the shack. The door swung open and discovered Sid McCoy sitting on a dirty bunk, head in his hands. He looked up as Hatfield entered, staring in amazement. The Ranger gagged at the awful stench of death and corruption that pervaded the place.

"Don't ask questions!" he shot at Sid as the latter started to speak. "Get out and get out quick."

McCoy needed no further urging. He leaped for the door and was outside almost as quickly as the Ranger. Instantly he swooped on the unconscious guard, ripped his gunbelt free and buckled it around his own lean waist.

"All right, feller," he snapped, "don't know where yuh come from, but I'm with yuh."

"That's the stuff," approved the Lone Wolf. "Tell you things later. Come on, follow me. How'd they come to wideloop you?"

"Was goin' to meet Karen Walters," McCoy replied tersely. "We been gettin' t'gether since that night in the Fust Chance. Nigger Mike Brocas come to me with a message to meet her over on the Regal by the rim of Devil Canyon. Nigger Mike and I rode over last night and a gang jumped us. Got the drap on me and rustled me inter this hole. Nigger Mike got away."

"He would," Hatfield commented cryptically. "Did you see how they brought you here?"

"Musta been through a tunnel or somethin'. They

blindfolded me and didn't take the rag off till I was in the boat. We come down some steps or somethin', though, jedgin' from the racket the hosses made and the way their noses was p'ntin' down. Got a notion I can jedge 'bout how far we come in the boat."

"You'd better be judging it right," Hatfield told him grimly. "Careful, now, if we can make it across this last open space, we have a chance."

They didn't make it. Halfway across and a yell soared up from the cave mouth; then the spang of a shot.

The bullet screeched between them as they dived for the shelter of the growth. Hatfield swore under his breath. They were still on the wrong side of the cave mouth and to attempt to pass it would be little short of suicide. His guns flickered from their holsters and he sent a stream of lead screeching toward the cave. Figures that were on the point of emerging tumbled back with yells and curses. A howl of pain sounded.

"Yuh got one, feller!" exulted Sid McCoy. "Lemme have the next one."

"There'll be plenty for both of us, and more than we want," Hatfield told him. "Keep down low. They have rocks to hide behind and all we have is leaves and branches."

Guns were blazing inside the cave mouth; bullets flicked through the leaves, knocked splinters from the brush, slammed against the stones. Hatfield and McCoy answered the fire, but the angle was bad and they could accomplish little.

"They'll get the range on us in a minute and coil our twine for us proper," the Lone Wolf muttered, stuffing cartridges into his empty guns.

"If I can jest get a couple more 'fore they do for me!" Sid McCoy prayed soulfully.

Hatfield held his fire, searching with his keen eyes for some effectual means of attack. Suddenly his jaw tightened.

"Hold onto the ground," he told McCoy. "Hell's going to bust in a minute or I'm mistaken!"

Lining sights on the squat little dynamite house he

cut loose with both guns. The reports blended in a
drumroll of fire. There were cracks in the walls of the
shack and Hatfield sent a stream of bullets through
those cracks.

Suddenly the boom of his guns was wiped away by
the hand of a terrific explosion. Numbed, deafened,
knocked flat to the ground by the mighty concussion,
the Ranger saw the power house dissolve in a vast mush-
room of yellowish flame and swirling smoke. For a
moment he lay unable to move hand or foot; then he
managed to raise himself on one elbow and stare with
dilated eyes at the terrible destruction he had wrought.

Where the powder house had been was only a yawning chasm in the river bank, and through this chasm
the waters of the stream were pouring in a thundering
flood.

Straight for the cave mouth roared the frothing tor-
rent. The despairing yells of the doomed guards
sounded thinly through the tumult. Several fought their
way to the entrance, but were swept back. Only one, a
tall, broad-shouldered figure, tore his way through the
swirling water, hurling to death a companion who
clutched at his arm. Hatfield instantly recognized the
sinewy form and surged to his feet, guns snapping up.

But his hands were numbed and shaking. With a bitter curse he saw the faceless man, unharmed, crash into
the brush and vanish up the canyon. He turned to help
McCoy to his feet.

The young rancher was dazed and bleeding, but
apparently not seriously injured. As Hatfield started to
speak, an ominous rumbling roar sounded from the
cavern mouth. For a moment Hatfield wondered, then
he understood. Seizing McCoy by the shoulder, he spun
him toward the river, now little more than shallow
pools and muddy wallows below the break in the bank.

"Across—get across to the other side!" he barked.

Floundering, staggering, reeling, they surged through
the shallows, waded the mud and clawed their way up
the steep farther bank. Behind them sounded muffled
roars and crackling detonations. The water from the

river had reached the pit of fire and was pouring into it. Crouched against the rock wall of the canyon, Hatfield and McCoy stared across the stream.

Suddenly the churning water boiled back from the cavern mouth, as by some terrific expanding force within the mountain. Then, after a frothing, swirling moment of spray and dashing waves, it roared inward again as if drawn by an equally terrific suction. There was a moment of comparative silence, a numbing instant of terrible suspense. Then abruptly the face of the cliff bulged outward as by the impact of a prodigious fist driving from the bowels of the earth. For a fraction of a second the rock wall withstood the blow, giving stubbornly under the terrific strain, then it split into jagged serrations. Malformed masses heaved sluggishly outward. Black smoke streaked with livid fire gushed from the blasted opening. Then a snow-white pillar of vapor shot out from the center, instantly inflating to voluminous billows, through which burst black masses of rock and hydraheaded rockets of flame.

With the roar of a thousand thunderclaps the whole face of the cliff fell outward. Tons upon tons of shattered rock crashed down from above, sealing the cave mouth, damming the stream a second time and sending it booming down its original bed. The fire monster within the mountain retired triumphant, grumbling and growling to himself. Little spirals of steam coiled up through the shattered masses, wisped away, vanished. The air cleared, and silence, save for the moan and sob of the stream, settled upon the gloomy gorge. Sid McCoy drew a deep breath and wiped the blood from his face.

"Feller," he said with conviction, "when it comes to openin' up hell yuh're a whizzer!"

"Come on," Hatfield told him with a grin, "the devil's still loose. Look, the way those rocks are scattered around in the water, I believe we can make it across to the other side without getting much wetter than we are now. We can't get any muddier!"

They made it across, not without a couple of sharp tussles with the swift current. Once across, it did not take the Lone Wolf long to pick up the trail of the man they were following.

"He's hustlin'," McCoy remarked, "easy to foller as a wagon track."

Hour after hour they forced their way through the growth, the gloom of the gorge lessening as they worked out of the hills and the walls lowered. Toward the last they slowed up and proceeded cautiously. McCoy suddenly uttered a sharp exclamation.

"There, over t'other side that blasted pine—see the hole in the cliff?"

"Uh-huh," the Ranger nodded, "and see the horses in the stalls built under the overhang—regular stable."

"There's my pinto," McCoy added. "Saddle and bridle hangin' right 'longside him."

Five minutes later both were mounted and riding slowly along the dark corridor that sloped gently upward through the cliff. They did not dare chance a light because of the possibility of ambush. Farther on were broad steps cut in the stone, over which the horses stumbled slowly. Then another stretch of smooth, rising floor and finally a gleam of pale light. A little distance from a narrow opening they dismounted and crept forward on foot.

The corridor opened onto a rocky stretch of low, broken hills that lipped the canyon. Cracks and fissures and yawning openings were legion.

"You could ride within ten feet of this slit and never notice it was any different from the rest," Hatfield grunted. "We've got to take mighty sharp notice of things hereabouts or we won't find this place again."

"I'm takin' notes," McCoy told him, "and I got a good nose for this sorta thing. Yuh reckon any of them back there come through alive?"

"Not a chance," Hatfield told him. His eyes were somber as he thought of the fate of the poor laborers trapped in the bowels of the fire mountain.

"Just the same, they're better off," he told himself. "They were good as dead anyhow, and the way they went out was quicker and a sight easier."

He shifted his throbbing left arm to a slightly more comfortable position.

CHAPTER XIX

THEY rode swiftly along the rim of the canyon until they reached the thicket where Hatfield had left Goldy. Here he slipped saddle and bridle from the piebald he had been riding and sent it skittering with a friendly slap on its rawboned haunch.

"Get going," he told the cayuse. "We turned your partners loose down below and the lot of you can take it easy for a while. Wait till I get that yellow-top of mine out of the brush," he said to Sid McCoy. "Then we're riding fast. I got business to tend to."

McCoy stared at him a moment but asked no questions.

They crossed the Regal wire not far from the lower box of Devil Canyon. McCoy glanced westward along the trail.

"Here comes somebody from the direction of Vegas," he remarked, "comin' fast, too. It's Highpockets Hilton!"

As the lanky deputy drew near he let out a joyous whoop.

"Hatfield! Jest the feller I was wantin' more'n anybody else! And Sid McCoy! Where in blazes did you come from?"

"What's up, Hilton?" the Ranger asked quickly.

"Nigger Mike Brocas come chargin' up to the Bar M," Highpockets exclaimed, "yellin' that Don Sebastian and his outfit had widelooped Sid and was gonna cash him in. Old Anse and Chet Madison and the rest of the outfit went boilin' over to the Regal hacienda to fight it out with the Lazy R outfit. They're there now and no knowing what all's happened. I sent

132

Doc Austin and Hogface Holliday to round up Dent Crane—he was up to the Cross-in-a-Box to see 'bout that sale. They'll be follerin' me quick as they get Dent."

The words were jolted out of Highpockets in chopped sections, for all three horses were already scudding the trail. Both Highpockets and Sid McCoy were well mounted, but the great sorrel steadily drew away from them. He was several hundred yards in front when the iron gate of the Regal ranchhouse yard appeared.

Long before it was in sight, the speeding trio could hear an ominous crackle like burning sticks, which steadily grew louder. Guns were banging away merrily when Hatfield swerved the blowing sorrel through the open gate. Behind trees in the yard crouched the Bar M waddies, aiming and firing. Flickers of flame answered from the windows of the Regal ranchhouse, where Don Sebastian and his men were barricaded.

Straight into the line of fire thundered the tall sorrel, the Ranger fumbling at his leather belt. He flung himself from the saddle and strode forward, stern, erect, guns swinging low on his muscular thighs, a silver star set on a silver circle gleaming on his left breast. He raised one slim hand and his voice thundered above the rising tumult—

"In the name of the state of Texas! Put up those guns and step forward! We've had enough of this nonsense!"

Turning he faced the big house.

"That goes for you fellows in there, too!" he boomed. "Come on out here. I've got plenty to say to all of you!"

There was a moment of tingling silence, then—

"Good gosh!" bellowed Chet Madison, "a Ranger!"

"Yeah," bawled Highpockets Hilton, jerking his horse to a sliding halt. "Yeah, a Ranger, and if any of you would like to know it—that happens to be the Lone Wolf! Ever hear of him?"

They had, not a man there who hadn't heard of the famous Lieutenant of Rangers, grim old Captain Bill McDowell's ace man. A second stunned silence, broken by Devil Anse McCoy's shrill yell—

"Sid! Where in the blankety-blank-blank did you come from? What *is* goin' on 'round here, anyhow?"

The front door of the Regal *casa* banged open and a girl came running out, red curls flying in the wind. Sid McCoy flung himself from the saddle and gathered her close in his long arms. Old Anse stared, gulped, turned his astounded eyes to meet the gaze of Don Sebastian Gomez, who was just coming down the steps, his men flocking behind him. Jim Hatfield glanced from one to the other, his eyes suddenly sunny, his firm lips quirking in a grin.

"Well," he drawled, "do you two still figger on keepin' it up and cheatin' some kids out of having great-grandfathers?"

Old Anse glanced at his tall grandson and the red-haired girl, glanced back to Don Sebastian. Don Sebastian suddenly smiled with a flash of white teeth. Old Anse grinned without any teeth at all.

"Well," he chuckled creakily, "I allus did have a hankerin' to be a great-grandpappy. Think ye can stand the strain, Gomez?"

Pedro Zorrila, standing near Karen Walters, fingered his scarred jaw reflectively.

"Remember what I said of being slapped by heem?" he asked the girl. "To me it happened, and I still think so."

Karen looked the foreman straight in the eye. "I haven't changed my mind, either," she said, and smiled up into Sid McCoy's face.

Hatfield was searching for a face among the crowd jostling about the yard. Suddenly his voice rang out, stern, peremptory.

"Halt, Brocas! Halt, I tell you!"

Nigger Mike Brocas, slinking furtively from tree to tree to where the horses were tethered, whirled with a curse. Flame streamed from the gun held in his one good hand; the bullet fanned Hatfield's cheek.

The Ranger shot him before he could pull trigger a second time. Nigger Mike went down in a floundering heap, the gun spinning from his hand. Hatfield walked over to him, took one glance at the blood-spouting wound, jerked Nigger Mike's shirt off and tore it into strips. He went to work on the half-breed with tourniquet and bandages. Nigger Mike stared up at him with dark, inscrutable eyes. Sid McCoy, understanding at last the part Nigger Mike played, was explaining the situation to the excited crowd. Nigger Mike continued to stare at the Ranger.

"Why you no let die?" he inquired at last. Hatfield smiled down at the wounded man, his eyes all kindness.

"I don't want to have you die, Mike," he said. "Maybe you didn't understand things. I had to stop you from tramping on other folks' toes."

Nigger Mike considered, glanced at his bandaged leg and nodded.

"Yuh a heap man," he said at length.

Hatfield squatted beside him. "Got a notion there's a good deal of man somewhere in you, too, Mike," he said softly. "I'd like to root it out. S'pose you tell me all about the bus'ness and let me try and figure things for you?"

Nigger Mike nodded. "Uh-huh, me talk."

A little later Hatfield rose to his feet, hitched his gunbelts a little and turned to Highpockets Hilton.

"Come on," he told the deputy, "you ought to be in on the last act of this show. No, I don't want you, Sid, or anybody else. You look after Mike till Doc gets here. Be seeing you in a little while."

Together he and the deputy sheriff rode north by east across the Regal range.

"Here," suddenly exclaimed Highpockets. "Here's that letter yuh left word with me to get to yuh. It come this mawnin', care our office."

Hatfield took the bulky envelope and tore it open. He read Captain Bill McDowell's letter and then unfolded the enclosure, glanced at it with satisfaction and stowed it away carefully, alongside the page he tore from Doc Austin's work on mineralogy and the note the bartender handed him the night of the big poker game.

"Last knot's tied," he observed cryptically, and quickened the pace of his horse.

Before the cool veranda of Cross P ranchhouse they dismounted. Nobody appeared to hold the horses, nor was there a greeting at the big front door. Hatfield pushed it open and strode into the house, the deputy close at his heels.

"Down anybody who starts anything funny," he flung over his shoulder to Highpockets. "I don't think we'll meet with anythin', but you never can tell."

Nelson Page was seated at the big desk. He turned his white, expressionless face to the opening door and his burning eyes took in the Ranger and his companion.

"To what am I indebted for this intrusion?" he asked, his voice calm.

Hatfield strode to the desk.

"*Trail's end, Paxton!*" he said as his hand shot forward.

The hand came back with a wrench and a twist, and with it came the exquisitely molded, flawlessly colored mask.

Noseless, almost lipless, scarred and distorted, was the face of the man behind the desk—flesh that was like slag from the furnace, withered and knobbed and gray, from out of which glared two eyes burning with the light of hate and madness.

With a wild curse, Nelson Page, who had once been Paxton, the prospector, moved his sinewy hands. Jim Hatfield hurled Highpockets from in front of the desk a split second before the twin barrels of the hidden shotgun roared. The charge crashed through the thin front broads of the desk, flicking wisps of hair from the Ranger's close fitting chaps. Page surged to his feet, hands flashing to his belt, his draw deadly smooth and lightning fast.

Hatfield's long Colt boomed, a trickle of smoke spiralled up from the muzzle. Page thudded forward upon the desk, rolled over sideways and fell to the floor. His eyes were already setting when Hatfield turned him over and raised his head. And the wild light had left his eyes, leaving in them the hurt expression of a bewildered child.

"I was mad!" he whispered. "I've been mad ever since it happened. I used to be a handsome man, but—but after it happened, women shuddered to look at me, and children would scream. You were right—on—the—mountain—"

Hatfield covered the scarred dead face with a handkerchief, rose to his feet and walked to the inner door and flung it open. Doctor Tsiang sat at the little table, an unstoppered vial beside him. The big Chinese nodded to the Ranger in a friendly way.

"Yes, he was mad," Tsiang said, nodding toward the outer room. "I cured him of his affliction, arrested its ravages before it could take his life, but I could not cure his mind. He befriended me, and dominated me."

Hatfield leaned forward eagerly. "You cured him? You can stop the working of the poison?"

Tsiang nodded. "Yes, I and I alone of all the world. A tedious and complicated treatment. I wish now that I had the time to impart the information to you—but, the secret dies with me."

He gestured toward the empty vial, smiled faintly and his magnificent head sank on his breast. He was dead before Hatfield could reach him.

The Ranger gazed steadily at the dead scientist, turned and glanced toward the still form on the floor.

"The worst thing of all that Paxton did," he said sadly, "was to destroy that brain before its time. Help me get this arm of mine in a sling, will you, Hilton?"

Chapter XX

SHERIFF CRANE was at the Regal ranch when Hatfield and Highpockets arrived. With him were Hogface Holliday and Doc Austin.

"How's Mike?" Hatfield asked, after the happenings at the Cross P had been related.

"Yuh can't kill him," grunted Doc. "Two tries and yuh failed up both times. Still waitin' for a hangin'."

"I figure there's something in him worth hanging onto," grinned Hatfield. "Take a look at this arm of mine, will you? Doesn't feel so good."

Old Doc bared the arm, glanced at the dark scab and grunted.

"Who the hell's been vaccinatin' yuh 'gainst smallpox?" he demanded. "Did a good job all right, but yuh been usin' the arm too much. Didn't it bother yuh?"

"It bothered me a sight more before I read about radium poisoning the other day in your office, and realized what he did to me was nothing but a bluff," the Ranger replied. "Yes, that's what was the matter with those poor devils from the river village, and Tom Hardy, and Page himself, who used to be Paxton—radium poisoning."

"Down there in Devil Canyon," he continued, "is one of the richest deposits of carnotite ore in the world. Carnotite ore is the source of uranium and, incidentally, radium, the new element which was discovered not so long back. Neal Paxton was an educated man, a mining engineer, before he turned prospector. He wrote some addresses and references in your books, Doc,—that was before the days he had anything to hide,—and Captain McDowell traced his early history easily. Nigger Mike

Brocas filled in some spots for me. Paxton recognized the fact that the Tinaja Hills are an almost identical formation to that of the La Sal mountains in Peru, which are good prospecting ground for carnotite and pitchblende. You know the first carnotite mining was done over on Roc Creek, way back in the early '80's. Paxton found those yellow carnotite and black vanadium outcroppings up in the Tinaja Hills and figured that down in Devil Canyon, at the base of the sandstone beds, there ought to be rich ore. He was right. He managed to get into the canyon, found the veins of ore, built a cabin up there and worked the beds. Also he figured out a better and quicker way of refining radium from the pitchblende than anybody else has so far. The only catch in it was that it laid him open to radium poisoning."

"That's what ate his face up, eh?" interjected Highpockets Hilton.

"Uh-huh," Hatfield nodded. "When he found out what was happening to him, he went nearly crazy. He left his mine and went to New York, leaving Nigger Mike Brocas to look after the workings while he was gone. He saved Nigger Mike from being hung over Arizona way and Mike stuck to him after that. I reckon he was near the end of his rope when he ran into Dr. Tsiang. Tsiang either cured him or at least managed to hold up the poisoning—only time could tell about that for sure. Paxton came back and found out that Don Sebastian had bought the Regal ranch while he was away and wouldn't sell. He tried to buy it through agents and couldn't. Right, Don Sebastian?"

"Yes," said Don Sebastian. "I had many offers for the property, but I wished it for a home and refused to sell."

"There he was," continued Hatfield, "knowing where there was a mine worth millions, and he couldn't get title to it. You know radium is worth around a hundred thousand dollars a milligram; but there's so little of it in the world that it is impossible to sell it without explaining where you got it. Just like some famous diamond. Paxton had to get title to the Regal."

"Where'd he get this mask with which to cover his deformity?" asked Don Sebastian, examining the exquisite workmanship of the thing.

"Tsiang made it for him," the Ranger replied. "Tsiang was a genius in more ways than one. Paxton came back west, bought the old Turner place and posed as an invalid. He always wore the mask when anyone came to see him and with that shadowy room of his it was hardly possible to tell it wasn't his real face. Every time he came to town, you'll recall, it was late in the evening or at night, and he always stayed in his buckboard."

Sheriff Crane and Hogface Holliday nodded agreement.

"Paxton was just about plumb loco, by then, I reckon," Hatfield continued. "He'd hit on the scheme of raiding the river villages for labor, and he was doing all he could to help along trouble between Don Sebastian and everybody else. That must have been his reason for widelooping Tom Hardy and then sending him back when he was nearly dead with the poisoning. He probably knocked off the men Don Sebastian missed, too. All the time he was posing as a friend to the Mexicans and Indians and pretending to have it in for white folks. He figured that would keep suspicion away from him. And all the time he was working the mine and storing up radium in the canyon."

"How'd yuh ketch onto him, Hatfield?" asked Hogface Holliday.

"When I went up to thank him and Tsiang for doctoring me I got the first notion," the Ranger replied. "That night I was shot, I got a good look at one of the jiggers I downed and saw he was a Chinaman. He was a northern Chinaman, mighty big and mighty dark; some folks might have taken him for a Mexican, but he had the drooping eyelids with the corners joined—the Mongolian apron, they call it. Nelson Page had Chinamen working for him, and Tsiang was Chinese. In that laboratory down in the canyon, I saw a set of silver fingernail guards, the kind high caste Chinese wear to protect their extra long fingernails when they do work with their hands. Tsiang was the scientist of the pair and Tsiang had the kind of fingernails I'm speaking about. All the other Chinese I'd seen around were low caste and wouldn't have any use for such things. It wasn't hard to figure it was Tsiang who was doing work in that laboratory."

He paused to roll a cigarette, drew a deep lungful of smoke and continued:

"I knew there was something funny about Page that first day I saw him when he laid his hands on his desk. They were big and packed full of muscle and all tanned and rough. The kind of hands a fellow staying in the house and sitting at a desk most of the time, as Page was supposed to do, wouldn't have. Widelooping me after I left the Cross P came in just a little too pat, too. They were anxious to make it look as though it were done by Don Sebastian's men. Having his men ride Lazy R horses they'd rustled was another idea to throw suspicion on Don Sebastian. Of course, they had to ride his range, because the cave entrance which Paxton found led into the canyon was there, another reason they rode Lazy R cayuses that wouldn't attract attention if they were seen. When the fellow with his face covered talked to me down in the canyon, I got a good look at his hands and they looked just the same as Page's hands. Then I saw that some of the guards down there were Chinese. It was all tying up. The night of the poker game, I knew that row was staged by somebody who didn't want the trouble between Don Sebastian and McCoy settled without a real fight that would end up by his having a chance to grab off the Regal. That night I got this note and it turned out to be the same handwriting as Paxton's in Doc's books, and the same as the letter Nelson Page wrote to Cap. McDowell asking for Rangers. Paxton slipped big there. Once I found out what was in the canyon, the rest was easy."

"And he vaccinated yuh to try to scare yuh inter joinin' with him, eh?" remarked Doc.

"Yes, that had me bothered for a while. He knew I was a Ranger and if he had me under his thumb I could do him a lot of good."

"That's where he slipped bad again," remarked Dent Crane. "Rangers don't scare."

"Anyhow, they try to keep from showing it," grinned the Lone Wolf. "Well, reckon that's about all. Only the carnotite ore's still down there in your canyon, Don Sebastian. Pity it can't be got out. Radium is doing an awful lot of good for sick folks and there isn't much of it."

Don Sebastian smiled. "Yes, it would be a fine thing to do," he said. "Perhaps, if I can raise money enough—"

"Now don't try to hawg all the chances they is for doin' good," growled old Anse. "I got a few pesos in the bank and I ain't gonna be able to take 'em with me when I step off 'fore long. Now—"

Don Sebastian extended a slim hand and they shook solemnly.

"And now," remarked Hogface Holliday, "I callate it's time to eat. Ridin' back with me, Jim?"

Hatfield smiled and shook his head. "No, I'm riding north," he replied. "Cap. Bill writes me there's something that needs looking into up around Cero Diablo."

"Good gosh!" exploded Dent Crane. "That's the hangout of the saltiest varmints in all Texas. I'd jest as soon ride inter a rattlesnake hole!"

The Lone Wolf nodded, and in his gray eyes was a look of pleasant anticipation.

THE END

Leslie Scott was born in Lewisburg, West Virginia. During the Great War, he joined the French Foreign Legion and spent four years in the trenches. In the 1920s he worked as a mining engineer and bridge builder in the western American states and in China before settling in New York. A bar-room discussion in 1934 with Leo Margulies, who was managing editor for Standard Magazines, prompted Scott to try writing fiction. He went on to create two of the most notable series characters in Western pulp magazines. In 1936, Standard Magazines launched, and in *Texas Rangers*, Scott under the house name of **Jackson Cole** created Jim Hatfield, Texas Ranger, a character whose popularity was so great with readers that this magazine featuring his adventures lasted until 1958. When others eventually began contributing Jim Hatfield stories, Scott created another Texas Ranger hero, Walt Slade, better known as *El Halcon*, the Hawk, whose exploits were regularly featured in *Thrilling Western*. In the 1950s Scott moved quickly into writing book-length adventures about both Jim Hatfield and Walt Slade in long series of original paperback Westerns. At the same time, however, Scott was also doing some of his best work in hardcover Westerns published by Arcadia House; thoughtful, well-constructed stories, with engaging characters and authentic settings and situations. Among the best of these, surely, are *Silver City* (1953), *Longhorn Empire* (1954), *The Trail Builders* (1956), and *Blood on the Rio Grande* (1959). In these hardcover Westerns, many of which have never been reprinted, Scott proved himself highly capable of writing traditional Western stories with characters who have sufficient depth to change in the course of the narrative and with a degree of authenticity and historical accuracy absent from many of his series stories.